GALLI

FROM DETECTIVE EMERSON'S FILES

BY PETER SAUNDERS

Published by Starry Night Publishing.Com

Rochester, New York

Copyright 2015 Peter Saunders

This book remains the copyrighted property of the author, and may not be reproduced, copied and distributed for commercial, or noncommercial purposes. Thank you for your support.

Peter Saunders

Contents

Dedication	5
Chapter 1: The Sacrifice	7
Chapter 2: The Pilgrimage	9
Chapter 3: A Small Happening	19
Chapter 4: The New Client	23
Chapter 5: Elizabeth's Last Request	27
Chapter 6: Bull	35
Chapter 7: Finding Patterns	41
Chapter 8: The Guest	49
Chapter 9: The Threat	55
Chapter 10: The Switch	61
Chapter 11: Lieutenant Jeff Keller	69
Chapter 12: Professor Rapin	75
Chapter 13: Luis Bertini	83
Chapter 14: Letting Go	89
Chapter 15: Michelle	93
Chapter 16: The Album	99
Chapter 17: Thomas Barkley	105
Chapter 18: Elizabeth's Diaries	109
Chapter 19: The Letter	113
Chapter 20: The Elusive Mr. Tucker, P.C.	121
Chapter 21: Message Received	127
Chapter 22: Finding Bull	131
Chapter 23: Bull's Dream	135
Chapter 24: The Lonely Night	139
Chapter 25: Seawood and Johnny L.	143
Chapter 26: The Rendezvous	151
Chapter 27: The Meeting	157
Chapter 28: Lost Childhood	163
Chapter 29: The Lead	169
Chapter 30: Prisoner in Love	175
Chapter 31: The Link	183
Chapter 32: Extending The Net	187
Chapter 33: Setting The Trap	191
Chapter 34: Encounter at the Hoeysunder Museum	197
Chapter 35: Elizabeth's Final Wish	207
Peter Saunders	209

Peter Saunders

Dedication

To Joan for all her support and more…

To our families of dreamers and survivors

And a special thanks

To Phyllis Eickelberg for being a perfect role model and for her literary support

Peter Saunders

Gallery of the Chosen

Chapter 1: The Sacrifice

Neils Vinter knew each blood sacrifice required spiritual preparation. Calming resonant tones would spread throughout his tense body as meditative music and the pure scent of sandalwood took him to where his uncontrollable urges were suspended in perfect balance. He sat crossed-legged on a Persian carpet facing his gallery of the chosen. Lining the walls of his chamber were framed prints of sacred paintings of beautiful women. The gods had chosen specific artists -- Waterhouse, Bouguereau, Lord Leighton, Burne-Jones, Godward and Alma-Tadema -- to capture ideals reflected in their flesh and blood models. Neils believed each painting fueled artistic inspiration. But he could see women were threatening such ideals through their willfulness and physical decay. And their refusal to serve the gods was turning the art world away from these dedicated artists and the ideals they represented through their paintings. As punishment, the gods demanded blood sacrifices. Attached to each print was a photograph of a beautiful female whom Neils had murdered and presented as an offering.

From each print, pure, virginal maidens peered down at him in adoration from their perfect worlds. As their protector and guardian, Neils could feel their deep love and devotion.

Visions swayed before him through flickering candlelight and shadows, crowding out the memory and the bloodied image of his foster mother as she lay dying on the kitchen floor. Even in death, she stared up at him with accusing eyes. *What good are you?*

Slowly the maidens peering down began speaking, drawing his attention, encouraging him to save their flawless worlds. In return, they offered their eternal beauty, obedience and redemption from his tormented childhood and all imperfections in his world.

Neils turned to face the poster of his favorite painting, *Dolce Far Niente* by Godward. Neils could feel his consciousness expanding, his mind reaching out to embrace the mysterious woman clothed in layers of light cotton as she lay on a tiger skin, her body curled, her dark eyes and supplicant body full of promise. Behind her, delicate lily pads floated on the still waters in a circular stone fountain. Time hung suspended, waiting.

Peter Saunders

Slowly Neils turned his gaze to the instruments that lay on the table before him. They were sacrificial knives; each with its elaborately decorated handle shaped in the form of an animal's head, each an exquisite work of art. With both hands, Neils lifted the knife with the horse's head. Closing his eyes, he visualized the futile struggle of his newly chosen offering, followed by the slow release of life as her warm blood spread over the steel blade and handle. He felt pleasure as he imagined the offering's warm blood bathing his hands.

As high priest and artist, Neils would humbly accept his victim's blood gift, while he completed the rite of sacrifice where imperfect flesh yielded to the source of all inspiration and beauty. Like the artists he worshiped, Neils would capture each woman's beauty at its peak and, with the razor sharp edge of his blade, prevent the corruption of her flesh. The ideal would be eternal.

He opened his eyes and scanned the two photographs carefully placed beneath each poster. The first photograph was taken from a distance without the offering's knowledge. He had studied that photo carefully, deciding if her beauty would be acceptable to the gods. Those chosen he would track down and perform his ritual.

The second photograph, taken moments after the violent, sacrificial act, showed the offering's face smeared with her own blood and a sample of her hair cut and taped over her eyes. Her arms were folded across her chest and her head tilted back. It was a rite Neils performed meticulously according to an ancient practice.

At the far end of his gallery hung a newly mounted poster of Waterhouse's Hylas and the Nymphs. In the poster, the nymphs stood waist deep among lily pads, their supple breasts testaments to eternal life, their eyes fixed on Neils, their guardian, their deliverer. All waited patiently knowing it would not be long before they would welcome his next human gift into their perfect world. Neils studied the single photo of a dark-haired woman sitting alone at a restaurant. Her name was Barbara Emerson and her beauty unmistakable. She would be his next offering, for she would please the gods.

Chapter 2: The Pilgrimage

Detective Ward Emerson had made his way up the steep hill to his therapist's office in the old colonial house many times, but today's session would be painful. He would have to revisit his wife's brutal murder and his emotional breakdown after two years of unsuccessfully searching for her killer. He climbed the stairs and paused at the front door. He should be hunting down his wife's murderer, not wasting time with therapists. But the depression that had set in weighed heavily on him. Since becoming a private detective, he had solved hundreds of cases. But this time was different; Barbara's death made it different. He had tried to numb his pain through booze, but that hadn't worked. He closed his eyes and pressed the buzzer. When the door clicked open, he slowly made his way down the hall to Dr. Cynthia Morgan's office. She greeted him as he entered and went directly to her chair. Ward removed his coat as he settled into the chair opposite, his heart pounding.

"How was your weekend?"

"So-so." Ward was middle age, muscular and lanky. His frosted sideburns and solid jaw gave him a distinctive appearance. Despite his jeans and badly wrinkled shirt, he had Westchester wealth written all over him.

Dr. Morgan waited, but Ward remained silent. "How about the drinking? Are you getting that under control?"

Ward took a deep breath. "I'm working on it."

"Good. Let's pick up where we left off." Dr. Morgan flipped through the pages of her thick notebook, her eyes scanning the entries. Cynthia Morgan was tall and thin. Silver hair curled softly around her face. She wore grey slacks and jacket with a white, scooped-necked blouse. "You said at our last session you felt you were responsible for your wife's death. You said, 'I believe Barbara paid a price I should have paid.' Do you really believe that?"

"I usually know when I've crossed the line, but not this time." He stared straight ahead, trying to focus.

"The line? What line are you referring to?"

"When you've been in this business as long as I have, you develop a sixth sense; you know when you're close to breaking open a case. There's a line, a point where if you cross it you can't turn back. Your life..." He stopped mid-sentence.

"Go on. What were you about to say?"

"There is a line and once you've crossed it you put your life and those close to you in danger. Before, I always knew when I was about to cross that line. I had time to weigh the risks and prepare, but not this time." He banged his fist on the chair's armrest. "Look, I don't see how all this talk is getting us anywhere. I just need something to keep me going till I'm back on my feet."

Dr. Morgan put down her notebook. "You can take pills, but they'll just numb you. And then one day when you think all is well, you'll find yourself still down this dark rabbit hole you thought you'd climbed out of."

Although Barbara was gone, Ward clung desperately to her memory. Six months passed before he could give her clothes away and empty the bathroom of her lotions. There were times he thought he saw Barbara in the mall or crossing the street down by the flower market. Late at night, when he heard the elevator doors open and footsteps nearing his apartment, he was sure Barbara would walk in. He wanted to wake up and discover the whole thing had been a horrible nightmare. They would laugh. He would hold her and tell her how much he loved her. He couldn't let go of her memory, not while her murderer was still at large.

At night, he found himself plagued by images of Barbara's bloody body, the rituals of her funeral, her burial, and the sickly, sweet smell of flowers around her grave. He remembered the sympathy cards that came and then stopped, solemn words spoken to comfort him and the awful silence of his apartment. Then a chilling emptiness took hold. The weight of the terrible loneliness and nightmares pulled him down like quicksand. He lost track of time and his memory failed him. Two friends, Michelle LaGrange and Tom Oliver suggested he see Dr. Cynthia Morgan, considered one of the best psychiatrists in Westchester County.

"Ward, do you want me to prescribe medications?"

Ward sensed his disapproving father looking on. He took a deep breath. "No, it's just that I didn't want to come here. In my family, if you had a problem you kept it to yourself and carried on."

"Whose idea was it to keep your problems to yourself?" Dr. Morgan jotted a note in her binder.

"My father's. He was an expert at avoiding life's problems. He would dismiss the topic with a wave of his hand, blaming mother for everything and anything that went wrong. Many times he would leave for the club and sometimes return after midnight in a state of rage looking for a fight."

"So avoiding life's problems didn't work for your father or your family."

Ward thought for a moment. "No, he used alcohol to escape. My father was a weekend alcoholic who abused his wife and children. He was addicted to schemes for getting ahead and beating the next guy who came along with more money, a bigger house, or a more expensive car. He never missed an opportunity to make a buck or take a risk, preferably at someone else's expense. In public, he wore a different face; he came across as a polished executive, but underneath he was cruel and driven."

"Avoiding problems doesn't work. That's probably why your father drank so much and was physically abusive. We'll discuss him at another time." Dr. Morgan paused briefly. "I'm sorry you don't see value in what we're doing. All of this digging is necessary. You have to trust me. Of course, you can stop the therapy if you want." She waited.

Ward shook his head. "No, let's keep going."

Dr. Morgan nodded and looked at her notebook. "I want to get back to what you were saying about crossing a line and knowing when someone's life may be in danger. How do you know when you're about to cross this line you speak of?"

Ward sat back and thought for a moment. "Usually there are little signs that tip you off, an uncomfortable feeling, or a crazy dream. Sometimes the people you are chasing get nervous and give you a sign. Most of the time it's pure intuition. I would not be alive today if I hadn't recognized these signs and knew I was about to cross that line. As I said, I would calculate the risks and prepare for what might happen next. But there weren't any signs this time." A cold chill shot through him.

"And because you didn't get these signs, these feelings, dreams or intuitions, you feel you are responsible for your wife's murder?"

"Maybe not directly, but as I said before, Barbara's murder had to be linked to one of my cases. There are a number of people who would like to get back at me for spoiling their operations. There must have been signs I didn't see. I was helping my friends on the police force track down a group suspected of moving drugs for one of the mafia families. I found them. The bust that followed pretty well disrupted operations. All of this happened a few months before Barbara was murdered. For all I know, they might have wanted to teach me a lesson." Ward stood up and walked to the window. He peered out at a small wood behind the house and the deepening darkness.

"You believe drug dealers murdered your wife?"

Ward faced Dr. Morgan. "Look, I don't know for certain who murdered Barbara, but right now what I'm suggesting is the only thing that makes any sense to me. It's the only thing I have to hang on to. I must be missing something, some link." Ward rubbed his forehead. "I can't seem to concentrate. I've always been able to break the cases I've worked on. It's ironic, isn't it?"

Cynthia looked a bit puzzled. "What do you mean?"

Ward returned to his chair. "I'm known as the private detective who solves cases others can't. If I find someone who has broken the law, I won't stop until I see justice done. Now, when it's my own wife who's involved, I seem helpless."

An image of his wife's bloody face and body flashed before him. Ward waited for the image to fade. "Some fucking detective! I screwed up big time. I thought I could protect her. I was so sure, so confident I had things under control, but I screwed up and Barbara paid the price. God, I love her so much."

"I can see that," Dr. Morgan said softly. "But is there any real proof? I mean is there any evidence at all that Barbara's death was the result of your work?"

Ward could feel his blood pressure rising. He shot back his response. "The murderer didn't leave a calling card, if that's what you mean." He turned and looked away indicating he was through discussing the topic.

Dr. Morgan turned to a new page in her notebook. "Ward, tell me how your wife died."

Tightness gripped his chest.

"Take your time."

Gallery of the Chosen

Ward shifted uneasily in his chair and took a deep breath. The setting sun cast shadows that swallowed the room. Dr. Morgan snapped on her desk lamp and a floor lamp near Ward's chair. Slowly Ward drifted back to the night of the murder.

"The night it happened, Barbara and I had planned to eat out and then go shopping. We liked to shop evenings when most customers had gone home and we have the full attention of the sales staff. But that night I was tied up in the city, so I called Barbara and suggested she go ahead without me and I would meet her at home. That was around 5 p.m. I was surprised she wasn't at the apartment when I arrived around 10 p.m. I called a few of her friends to see if they had gone with her. But no one had seen her. By 11 p.m., I was heading out for the department store when I received a call from Captain Bill Travers of the New Rochelle Police. They had found Barbara's body by the pond at the Glen Island Casino Park. I didn't wait to hear what else Travers had to say, but hung up and raced to the park.

"No God, please, it can't be her." Ward ran from his car and past an officer who tried to stop him from entering the crime scene. Some officers were standing, others kneeling as they circled Barbara's body. Medical personnel were preparing the body bag. They turned as Ward pushed past them. Captain Travers called out. "Ward, wait, don't. . . ." Ward reached Barbara's bloodstained body and held her in his arms until two officers pulled her from him. Her face and chest were covered with blood.

For a moment, the ticking of Dr. Morgan's clock was the only sound in the room. Ward finally continued, "There was no sign of attempted rape; her money and credit cards were still in her purse. Barbara's throat had been slashed and her blood smeared across her forehead and down her cheeks. Whoever murdered her did so for a reason. The way her face was marked with her own blood suggested she was murdered as part of a ritual."

Dr. Morgan watched Ward closely as his breathing became more labored.

"Are you okay?" She leaned toward him.

He nodded. "Yes, but I don't know if I can continue." He wiped tears from his eyes with the back of his hand.

"You can do this, Ward. Keep going."

"The security video taken at the department store's underground parking garage shows Barbara's car pulling into the parking garage three hours before she was murdered. Right after her car enters the garage, a van is seen following. The van drives past Barbara's car and parks in the next aisle. After Barbara parks and enters the department store, the driver pulls his van into an adjacent space. Whoever was in the van sat waiting. All we see is Barbara eventually returning to her car and moving between it and the van. There is nothing more to see. Both the car and van were in the shadows. From the bruises on her arms and legs, it is clear she was forced into the van. I believe she was targeted."

Ward paused, lowered his head then slowly raised it and continued. "A short time passed and then the van pulled away. A few days later the van was located, abandoned, across town. It had been stolen from a nearby car lot. A man who lives near the lot spotted a tall guy in a nylon tracksuit walking around the premises late one night. The video at the lot confirms what he saw. The suspect had the hood of his jacket up, so we don't get a good look at his face. That's all we have. Later, when the van was recovered, Barbara's blood was discovered on the van's walls and floor. She was murdered in the van and her body dumped at the park. Barbara had put up a good fight. Some of the killer's skin and blood were found under her fingernails, but the forensic people haven't been able to find a match."

Ward paused. The room was dark now except for the faint light cast by the lamps. The only sound breaking the heavy silence was the ticking clock.

"Is there anything else you can remember?" Dr. Morgan leaned forward.

Ward ran his fingers through his thick hair. "One more thing. Barbara's eyes were still open when I reached her." Ward looked helplessly across at his therapist. "There was something in her eyes I had never seen before."

"What was it?" Dr. Morgan's voice was almost a whisper.

Ward waited for the words to come. "A look of regret. There was a look of regret in her eyes. She was already dead. That's all I remember."

"At our last session you told me you had some trouble with the police investigating your wife's murder. Do you want to tell me about that?"

Ward covered his face with both hands, leaning his elbows on his knees. He looked up. "After a month of intensive searching, we had nothing, and Barbara's murderer was still out there. I could tell the officers were losing interest and had to move on to other things. As I've said, I suspected her murder was payback for one of the cases I was working on. The most likely candidate was a mafia family, the Gerberti. They have been entrenched in Brooklyn and Long Island for decades and were working to set up shop in Westchester."

"Did your colleagues at the force agree with you?"

Ward looked toward the window and the evening darkness outside. "No, they insisted that angle had been checked out and they couldn't find a link."

"And you didn't agree with the conclusion they reached?"

"No, I didn't. So I set up a meeting with an informant we had used. If the Gerberti had a contract on my wife, he would know or could find out. No one on the force knew what I was doing. I asked my contact to check. Later he said as far as he could discover, none of the families had anything to do with Barbara's murder. He said he couldn't help me."

"And you didn't believe him?"

"No. I was pretty sure this guy had answers I was looking for, so I leaned hard on him to see if that would help his memory, but then I . . . I lost control." Ward paused.

"What happened?"

Ward looked directly at Dr. Morgan. "I beat him with my pistol. I put the barrel of my gun into his mouth and told him he had one minute to tell me the truth."

Dr. Morgan sat motionless. "Did you kill him?"

"No. He just kept begging, saying he was telling the truth. I pulled the gun from his mouth and kept hitting him till he became unconscious. He almost died from internal bleeding. I am not proud of what I did."

"What happened to the informant?"

Ward shook his head. "Nothing. A friend on the force smoothed things over. In fact, the beating helped establish the punk's credibility. There was some suspicion among the families that he was working with us, but the kind of going over I gave him cleared him of suspicion. You might say I did him a favor. As I said, I lost control. It wasn't like me. It was a stupid thing to do. I jeopardized not only the guy's life, but also our whole delicate relationship with informants. I just lost it and went crazy. Barbara was my life."

"Now do you think the informant was telling you the truth?"

"Yes. No. Maybe. I don't know what I think. But I do know that the Gerberti family is the only one that had a strong enough motive for killing her. I'll get whoever did this."

Dr. Morgan studied Ward. "Are you working on other cases? I think it would be good for you to keep busy with other cases, nothing too heavy or dangerous, just something to give your mind some relief from the constant struggle to solve Barbara's case. It would help keep you away from drinking."

Ward gave no response.

"Will you think about what I've said?"

"I'll think about it."

Dr. Morgan looked at the clock on her desk. "Our time is almost up. Is there anything else you want to tell me?"

Ward stared at his therapist as if he wanted to say something but couldn't find the words.

"Ward, there is something, isn't there? What is it?"

"I don't know how to explain what I'm about to tell you. You'll think I'm nuts."

"What do you mean?"

"On the night of the murder as I drove back to New Rochelle from the city, planning to join Barbara at home, I thought I heard her speaking to me. I mean I heard her voice. It was so real."

"What did your wife say?"

Ward took a deep breath. "She said 'I love you. Don't worry.' I pulled to the side of the road and sat trying to figure out what I'd just heard."

"Are you sure it was Barbara's voice?"

"Yes."

"Did she say anything else?"

"No, that was all. I'm not sure what to make of this. You are the only person I've told. From where I sat on the side of the highway, I could see a big clock on the side of a building. So I noted the time when I had heard her voice and pulled over. Barbara had already been dead thirty minutes."

Peter Saunders

Chapter 3: A Small Happening

Ward and Barbara Emerson's favorite Friday evening hangout had been the Two Toms Tavern up on the old Post Road in New Rochelle. The tavern was the kind of watering hole that attracted and welcomed one and all. Boaters, firemen, police officers and small business owners rubbed elbows with doctors, lawyers and corporate executives. The recently divorced liked the tavern because they could drink freely away from their neighbors' curious eyes and swap woeful tales. Much comfort was found in the soulful voice of Michelle LaGrange, a French Canadian, who performed R&B on weekends. The tavern was a haven from expectations, those of others and one's own. And right now, Ward needed just such a place to escape his unsuccessful search for his wife's killer.

After Barbara was murdered, Ward's visits and drinking increased. Tom, the head bartender, knew when to pour a stiff drink and when to water one down. It was rumored he had been a top executive on Madison Avenue who cracked under the strain, hit the bottle and then the streets. His nephew, Tommy, helped him face his addiction and his demons. It was Tommy's idea to open a tavern together and his creative talent that made it popular.

Tom had been to hell and back and those who frequented his tavern respected him. If Tom demanded someone's car keys, no matter how important, tough or big the person might be, the keys were handed over without argument. The two Toms knew all the signs of who was on a drinking binge and who was close to falling into an alcoholic abyss. They placed Ward in this second category and watched him closely. Right now they were watering Ward's drinks. Ward knew it, but didn't mind.

There are small happenings in life that at first go unnoticed, happenings that seem insignificant but later change everything. This evening just such a small happening would change the course of Ward's life.

"Hey, Sherlock, how goes the snooping business?" Tom asked as he pulled a note from his vest pocket, leaned across the bar and handed it to Ward.

"What's this, last month's bar bill?" Ward joked.

"Your bill wouldn't fit on paper that small," Tom ribbed. "There was a young woman in earlier looking for you."

"Did she say what she wanted?"

"No." Tom lifted a glass and inspected it for water stains as he rubbed the rim with a bar towel. "She looked a bit nervous and uncomfortable." Tom poured Ward a Guinness and placed the glass in front of him. "I don't think she's ever been in a tavern before. She asked if I would give this note to you."

Ward unfolded the note,

Mr. Emerson:

Lieutenant Keller gave me your name. He said you might be able to help me with a family matter. Please call me at 212-555-6534.

Susan King

"How old was she?"

Tom smiled, picked up another glass and inspected it. "Twenty, maybe twenty-two, but you can forget it. She was too young and too smart for someone like you. She was more my type."

Ward smiled and stared at the note. A part of him wanted to toss it away. The tavern was his refuge from the world and its problems and he resented this intrusion. Why did his friend Jeff Keller give this kid his contact information? It was not like Jeff to do that. There had to be a really good reason. Ward stared at the note. Maybe this would be a simple assignment. Maybe he could knock it off in a few days and pay some of his bills. Besides, until there was a breakthrough in Barbara's case, his therapist suggested he keep busy.

Michelle had started singing in the next room and Ward felt the softness of her voice sweep over him. It was two years since his wife's death, and friends, sensing he was attracted to Michelle, suggested he ask her out. Ward had to admit she had a great figure and beautiful black hair that reached her waist, and a voice that went right to his soul. But he told himself he wasn't ready.

When Michelle had finished her song, Ward headed for the public phone and dialed Susan's number.

"Hello." The voice was young, soft and tentative.

"This is Ward Emerson. You wanted to see me?"

"Yes, thank you for calling. Lt. Keller said you could help me with a family matter." There was a long awkward pause. "Mr. Emerson is there someplace we can meet? I don't feel comfortable talking about this matter on the phone."

"Do you live in New Rochelle?"

"No, I live on Long Island, but I'm staying with friends in New Rochelle. I drove out hoping you would see me. It would mean a great deal to me and my family."

He sensed desperation in her voice.

Michelle had started her next song and Ward wanted to get back. He agreed to meet Susan at his office on Tuesday. Hanging up the phone, he returned to the bar, grabbed his drink and went into the lounge. Michelle looked his way and smiled as he slid into a seat. He took a long drink and could feel the rich, bitter taste do its magic on his tired bones. Ward looked at Susan's note and slid it into his shirt pocket. Tomorrow he might be drawn into someone's personal mess, but tonight he would just float on the tide of Michelle's sweet voice.

Peter Saunders

Chapter 4: The New Client

Narrow strips of sunlight framed drawn blinds in the darkened room where Ward lay asleep on a couch. The sound of a street door opening and slamming shut drifted up from below but did not disturb the sleeper. Downstairs, heavy footsteps shuffled across the creaking floor to the stairs and made a labored ascent followed by a determined rush to Ward's office door. A heavy but short man's silhouette filled the door's frosted glass panel. The doorknob turned but the door did not open.

"Crap. Ward, wake up. Get up. It's Bull. Open the door." Ward didn't move.

Finally, a key rattled in the lock and the door flew open, crashing against the wall as the visitor entered and hit the light switch. An overweight man in his twenties wearing a dark, busting-at-the-seams sports coat, white shirt, narrow tie, grey sweat pants and running shoes, stood in the doorway with a takeout coffee in one hand and the office door key in the other. His eyes fixed first on Ward and next on the mess of file folders, empty food containers and coffee cups scattered over the carpeted area.

"Double crap." Bull quickly put the coffee on the table in front of the couch, then rushed to the window and snapped open the blinds.

Sunlight streamed over Ward, prompting a mumbled "Who's there?" as he began to stir. Ward, unshaven, wore black jeans and a badly wrinkled grey tailored shirt. A yellow tie was mashed into his shirt pocket.

"Get up, it's me. Who else would it be? Get your butt off the couch." Bull removed his jacket and tossed it on a leather chair, then grabbed an overflowing trashcan next to the desk and an empty bottle of scotch from the floor and quickly hid both behind the drapes. Collecting files off the floor, he threw them on the desk.

"Boss, get up. Your new client will be here in. . . ." He glanced at his watch. "Hell! In twenty-five minutes. Get up. Go wash your face and comb your hair."

Ward slowly dragged his body off the couch and moved unsteadily toward a small bathroom off to one side. "Who in heaven's name is coming at this hour of the morning?"

Bull laughed as he dropped another pile of folders on the desk. "You're a detective. You're supposed to know who's coming. You read Susan King's letter, right?" No response from Ward. Bull straightened up and stared at his partner as he emerged from the bathroom, wiping his face with a washcloth.

"Crap! You didn't read her letter, did you?" In a panic, Bull tossed the files off the desk, back onto the floor till he found the letter.

Ward dropped down heavily on the couch. He put the wet washcloth across his forehead, closed his eyes and leaned back resting his head. "That feels better. Why would anyone want to come at this time of the morning?"

"It's three in the afternoon." Bull scanned the letter. "Okay. Here's what the letter says:

Dear Mr. Emerson, Thank you for agreeing to see me. Lieutenant Keller said you're the best detective he knows, and I would not be disappointed. I need your professional help with a family matter. I will explain everything when we meet. Susan King."

Bull stared at Ward. "Ring a bell?"

"Vaguely. She doesn't tell us much about her predicament."

"No, she doesn't. Why did you agree to see her? Shouldn't we hold out for a bigger case, one that might put us in the headlines?"

Ward removed the washcloth, turned it over and replaced it on his forehead. "Keller's a good friend and if we can do him a favor we should. Besides, I can tell you from experience that the big cases are rare; it's the smaller cases that are more interesting. Wait till you see what Miss King wants before you decide to write her off."

Bull didn't respond, but puffed out his cheeks in frustration as he gathered up more files and papers, piling them back on the desk. Then he grabbed a broom and began sweeping the take-out containers from the rug toward the closet door. Opening the door he pushed what he had collected into it, then shut the door.

Gallery of the Chosen

Bull surveyed the office. "This place is still a mess. It needs a major facelift if we want to send the right message and attract quality clients. First impressions are everything. I read that in an article for people on the move. Successful people dress smartly. We're walking billboards; that's what the author said."

Ward lifted the washcloth and peered curiously at Bull. "We're what?"

"Walking billboards. That's what the guy wrote and he's a highly respected authority on men's fashions. He's dressed hundreds of successful men on Wall Street."

"Billboards?"

"Yes, I mean what message would you say my billboard sends to the world?" Bull pushed out his broad chest, pulled in his protruding stomach, put his hands on his hips, and smiled. "I mean, my shirt and tie and jacket all say something powerful, don't you think?"

Ward put the washcloth back over his eyes. "I'm not quite sure what your billboard says."

"I'll tell you. It says I am confident and strong. In case you didn't notice, my pants are casual and say 'here's a sporty, regular, fun guy.' My shirt and jacket say 'although he's open to fun, he's fashionable, savvy and serious.' Good description, huh?"

Ward didn't remove the washcloth. "They say all that?"

"Of course."

"What does your tie say?" Ward challenged.

"That's obvious, Boss. It says 'although Mr. Toolman is strong and savvy and capable of having a good time, he's modest.' My tie is under…under…something." Bull rubbed his chin, something he did when stressed, confused or deep in thought.

"Understated?"

Bull's face lit up. "That's right! My tie is understated. Once you learn to read the messages I'm sending, you'll see I'm a confident man on the move. That's me all over."

A smile flickered briefly on Ward's face and then disappeared.

Bull's body snapped to attention as he heard the street door open and close. He glanced at his watch. "We're not ready. She's early. She's not supposed to be early. Why would she want to be early?" Beads of sweat appeared on Bull's forehead, as a look of desperation spread across his face.

"Maybe she's one of those rare creatures who is actually on time for appointments." Ward removed the washcloth. He noticed Bull staring at the door as if he expected a monster to walk through it at any moment. "Don't worry, we're ready. Put your coat on and sit down."

Bull grabbed his coat and struggled with it while he rushed to the wall switch and lowered the lights. "Maybe she won't notice the pig sty we work in."

Ward moved from the couch to one of the leather chairs facing the couch. "Try to show some interest in whatever she's come to us for. Your reputation as my brilliant assistant is at stake here, not to mention the fact that Miss King could bring in some much needed cash for our empty pockets. I don't believe I've paid you in some time, have I?"

"You owe me two month's salary." Seating himself in the remaining chair across from the couch, Bull turned to face Ward. "You do the talking; I'm nervous." A bead of sweat rolled down his left cheek.

Ward tossed the washcloth to his partner who quickly mopped his own face before stuffing the cloth under his seat cushion. Ward took a drink of his coffee. "Relax. We'll be fine."

The sound of footsteps reached the office door. The outline of a slender figure appeared in the frosted glass.

Ward deliberately raised his voice so the visitor at the door could hear what he was saying. "So this case is closed. You did a great job, Vincent. I understand you have that report completed."

Bull's eyes widened in panic. He shook his head from side to side, meaning he had no idea what Ward was talking about. Ward pointed to the files on the desk and signaled Bull to get him a folder, any folder. Bull quickly grabbed a file folder and handed it to Ward who opened it on the table in front of him.

There was a gentle knock on the door.

Ward smiled, "Come in."

Chapter 5: Elizabeth's Last Request

Susan King slowly opened the door and peered into the office. "Mr. Emerson?" She waited until Ward nodded his greeting.

"Yes. Please come in, Miss King. We were expecting you." He smiled as the young woman stepped into the room. Bull's mouth dropped open. Susan King was pretty—very pretty. A delicate gold cross and chain hung from her neck and draped a royal red mini-dress covered with delicate white flowers. A matching red headband accented long brown hair that settled below her shoulders. White leather boots reached to her shapely thighs. A white raincoat hung over her right arm while her left hand clutched a small red purse. She wore no makeup. She didn't need any. Twenty-two year old Susan King was someone not to be ignored.

Ward glanced at Bull who stared at the beautiful apparition before him. "Vincent, why don't you take Miss King's coat?"

Bull seemed to be in a daze. "What?"

Ward tilted his head toward their visitor. "Miss King's coat?"

Bull's body suddenly shot out of his chair as if he had just discovered he was sitting on a tack. "Yes." As he took her coat, Bull indicated Susan should sit on the couch.

"Can my partner get you something to drink?" Ward inquired.

Susan sat down and looked up at Bull. "A glass of water would be wonderful." Bull nodded vigorously as if a glass of water would indeed be just about the most wonderful thing anyone could request. He hurried with her coat to the closet and opened the door, but quickly closed it again to hide the garbage on the floor. His face turned a pinkish hue as he hung her coat on an old corner rack. He then went to a small table against a wall and poured water from a jug into a glass. He selected a paper napkin, scurried back and carefully put the glass on the napkin demonstrating that Vincent Toolman appreciated the finer points of social etiquette.

Susan gave Bull a half smile. "Thank you."

Ward noticed Susan's hand shaking slightly as she sipped from the glass. Deep lines on her face suggested many sleepless nights. Ward began, "This is my partner, Vincent Toolman."

Bull flashed Susan his widest smile as he squeezed himself back in the chair and adjusted his tie and jacket.

Ward continued, "Let me begin by saying that anything you say will be kept confidential. Now then, what can we do for you, Miss King?"

"Thank you for seeing me." Susan briefly looked away and then made eye contact with Ward. "Lieutenant Keller told me you might be able to help me."

"How do you come to know Lieutenant Keller?"

"My boyfriend just graduated from the Police Academy and now works for him. I hope it was okay for me to contact you?" As she spoke, one hand played with the chain around her neck. "You'll have to forgive me. I am a little nervous. I've never done anything like this before."

"And what would that be?"

"Why, hire a detective." Susan whispered the word 'detective' as though she were sharing a deep secret. "My boyfriend thinks I'm wasting your time. He wanted to come today, but I told him I wanted to do this myself. I hope you won't think me crazy, I mean, this isn't about a murder or robbery. It's about my grandmother."

The sound of a truck starting up startled Susan, drawing her attention to the window. She waited a moment, then turned back and continued. "Since my grandmother died I've had difficulty sleeping and when I do sleep…" She paused and started again. "When I do sleep, I have trouble staying asleep. I need your help."

Ward and Bull exchanged glances. "Susan, why don't you tell us what your problem is and let us decide if we can help you? Take your time."

"I don't know where to start. This is about my grandmother. But I told you that already, didn't I?"

Ward nodded.

"I've lived with her ever since my mother and father divorced."

"When was that?"

"Twelve years ago." Susan stared at her hands as she spoke. "My grandmother died recently after a series of strokes. We knew she didn't have long to live."

"We're sorry for your loss," Bull offered.

"Thank you. I guess no one's really prepared when the final moment comes."

"No, I guess we never are," Ward added. An image of mourners standing at his wife's gravesite flashed briefly in his mind, then faded.

"Elizabeth was a very private woman." Susan cleared her throat. "She liked me to call her by her given name. She said she felt old when I called her grandmother. It's important that you understand that she was very logical and her mind was clear. She was not emotional like me. You both must believe me about this."

"We understand."

"The doctors at Saint Michaels Hospital did everything they could. I'm sure of that."

"So this isn't about medical negligence?" Ward asked, trying to help Susan focus.

"No, no. It's about my grandmother's last request. A few hours before she died, Elizabeth begged my family not to bury her in the family plot. She seemed frightened about something."

Ward took a deep breath. He had little patience for sad-sack cases and normally would strangle anyone who sent such cases his way. But something told him to dig deeper. "Did Elizabeth indicate why she didn't want to be buried with the family?"

"Not really. Later, when I was alone with her at the hospital, she said it was something between her Maker and herself, a burden she must bear."

Bull gave Ward a mystified look as he shifted in his chair.

"Who else was in the room and heard Elizabeth make this request?"

"My great-uncle Paul and my mother, Angela. They were both there. It wasn't like Elizabeth to be frightened or to make such a strange request." Susan started to play with the chain around her neck again, but when she saw Ward watching her, she quickly put her hand in her lap.

"I see. Susan, may I call you by your first name?"

She fixed Ward with her eyes and hesitated for a moment. "I guess so."

"Susan, I've discovered that people who are dying say all kinds of strange things. Sometimes it's drugs that bring it on; sometimes it's anger or fear of dying."

"Maybe, but that's not how it was with Elizabeth. She wasn't a raving old woman pumped up on drugs." Susan raised her voice, her eyes challenging Ward. "I've told you, Elizabeth was very clear-headed before she died. She was a very religious woman and not afraid of dying. She was a very strong woman."

"I see. What did your uncle and mother think of Elizabeth's request?"

Susan's face went rigid. "My mother said Elizabeth was out of her mind, but that's a lie!" Susan's eyes flashed in defiance.

Bull joined in. "So, Elizabeth's request came out of the blue?"

Susan snapped back. "All I know is she didn't discuss it with me. I don't know what she might have said to my mother or my uncle. Elizabeth was pretty traditional. She didn't approve of my mother walking out on my father and me for another man. My dad took it pretty hard and hated giving me up to Elizabeth, but he was having a tough time financially, what with the divorce and all. The important thing is that my grandmother was in her right mind despite what my mother and uncle are saying. Why won't anyone believe me?" Without warning, Susan picked up her napkin, crumpled it, and threw it across the table and onto the floor. "

Bull stared wide-eyed at the crumpled napkin.

Ward jumped in. "Susan, we're just trying to understand what happened. We believe you."

Susan blushed. "Sorry. Sometimes I have a tough time controlling my temper. I've been having a difficult time since my grandmother died. I miss her."

Ward's own empty life echoed in Susan's words. And there was something about Susan King's determination, gentleness and beauty, which reminded him of his wife. "I understand. I lost my wife not long ago. It's hard to lose someone you care deeply for. You say your grandmother was frightened?"

Susan nodded. "Terrified would be a better way to describe her. She kept begging us over and over not to bury her in the family plot. She said she had saved some money and we should use it to buy a new plot."

Bull jumped in. "Did your mother and uncle grant Elizabeth her final wish?"

With a defeated look on her face Susan continued, "I couldn't persuade them to honor her request. They buried her with the rest of the Dwyer family."

Ward went to his desk, picked up a pad of paper and a pen, and then returned. "What family members are buried there?"

Susan thought for a moment. "My great-grandparents on my mother's side are there, and Elizabeth's brothers Albert, Edward and Pete. Elizabeth's husband, Todd Dixon, is also buried there. Elizabeth is the seventh." Susan opened her purse and removed a piece of paper. She pushed it across the table.

Ward and Bull leaned forward and read the note. *Mrs. Elizabeth Dwyer Dixon, Holy Ghost Cemetery, Seawood, Long Island.*

"Susan, is it possible your grandmother didn't want her final resting place to be next to someone she...," Ward hesitated, searching for the best way to say what he had to say. "Was there some family member she might have harbored angry feelings for, a brother, mother, even her husband?" He watched her face closely looking for telltale signs of the truth.

Susan hesitated. "I lived with her most of my life. We were very close. If she'd held such strong feelings against her relatives, she would have said something, but she didn't. She was terrified of something else."

"I see. Well, what exactly would you like us to do?"

"I want to know why Elizabeth made that strange request and why she was so frightened. She kept begging me to help her, but I can't help her unless I know why she was so scared. My mother demanded one good reason Elizabeth should not be buried with the other family members." Susan paused, tears welling up in her eyes. "I couldn't think of one so Elizabeth was buried with the rest of the family. I feel I've failed her, Mr. Emerson. I owe her for all the things she did for me over the years."

Ward took a deep breath. "Susan, these kinds of investigations are rarely successful. Family secrets have a stubborn way of staying secret. Relatives don't like strangers, especially private detectives, poking their noses into their business. Do your mother and uncle know you want to hire a detective?"

Susan looked down. "No, they don't know."

"You understand that your mother and uncle may be our best and only source for information. But from what you've told us, I suspect they won't be much help. And they may make your life miserable."

"I've thought of that, but I'm a big girl. I can handle myself."

"Still, if they don't cooperate, our chances of finding out what it is you want to know are very slim. We may never know why your grandmother made that request."

"Maybe they won't cooperate, but please understand that I have to try."

Ward nodded. "Yes, you have to try. You said your grandmother was at Saint Michaels Hospital." Ward jotted a note in his pad. "Where is that?"

"On Long Island at Seawood."

Ward glanced briefly at Susan as she reached into her purse and pulled out her checkbook. He held up a hand. "Susan, let us check out a few things and if we think there's a chance of finding what you want to know then we can talk about our fees. Meanwhile, if you think of anything that might shed light on this, like an unusual comment Elizabeth may have made, or anything at all no matter how insignificant, give us a call." He handed her his card.

Over the years Ward had learned how to deal with clients with hopeless cases. Normally he would make a few phone calls and, if everything dead-ended, he'd call the client back and tell them he had found no evidence to suggest they proceed. That was enough for most people. They had tried to do something for their loved ones and that was all anyone could ask. Ward didn't make any money this way, but if he could ease someone else's pain, he did. There was enough of it going around.

Susan gave him a slight smile and put her checkbook away. "Thank you both."

Bull retrieved Susan's coat and held it as she slipped into it. As Bull sat down, Susan walked to the door, hesitated, then she turned retracing her steps and sat down.

They waited.

"Elizabeth kept having a nightmare," Susan said in a half whisper. "It wouldn't leave her alone. She would wake up screaming and call to me in a panic."

"Go on."

"I would find her sitting upright in bed staring into space, begging someone to go away. I would put my arms around her and tell her no one was going to hurt her. When she calmed down, she would say it was just a bad dream, but I suspected there was something else, something so terrible she couldn't bring herself to talk about it."

"Did she ever describe the nightmare to you?"

"Yes, once. The dreams were always the same. She said there was a long dark hallway and at the far end she could see the silhouette of someone waiting, a man. He never spoke, but she said she knew it was a man. Then he started coming toward her and that's when she would scream begging him to go away."

"And did he?" Bull asked.

"I don't know. When the man reached the end of the hallway the dream always ended."

"So Elizabeth gave no clues about what this man looked like or who he might have been."

"No, she said he remained in the shadows as if waiting for something or someone."

A video clip from the underground parking surveillance camera flashed suddenly across Ward's memory, a clip he had reviewed a thousand times. A van is parked next to his wife's car; a dark figure sits waiting. Barbara walks from the department store's exit to her car amid shadows and faint light. She walks into the shadows between the van and her car and is gone forever.

"Elizabeth couldn't shake this dream."

Ward sat staring into space.

"Mr. Emerson?"

Ward looked at Susan and then at his notes. "Could Elizabeth's nightmare be somehow connected to her last request?"

Susan shrugged her shoulders. "I'm not sure. The night before she died, she fell into a deep sleep. I stayed with her, sitting by her bed, but I dosed off. Then I was awakened by a scream. She had that same terrified look on her face and was begging someone to leave her alone. I tried to comfort her, but she wouldn't take her eyes off the wall. I told her everything was all right, but she wasn't listening. All she said is 'he's waiting.'

"The night nurse arrived and gave Elizabeth something to calm her down. She went back to sleep and died early the next morning." Susan looked at Ward and then Bull. "Please, I can't do this by myself. Please help me."

Ward and Bull exchanged brief glances. Ward nodded. "Of course, we'll help you, if we can."

Susan walked over and gently took Ward's left hand in hers. The warmth and softness of her touch flowed through him, touching his heart.

"I'm sorry. I know how you wife died, how she was murdered. My boyfriend showed me the newspaper articles. You too have suffered a terrible loss. Did they ever catch her murderer?"

Ward said nothing, cleared his throat, breaking the awkward silence. "No. Barbara's killer is still out there."

Chapter 6: Bull

Ward's neck and back ached. He opened one eye, focusing on the nightstand clock: 6 a.m. Another evening had passed without much sleep. Hours of digging through FBI and county files on past homicides left his mind racing and his body exhausted. He had gone through these files several times before with little results, but his intuition told him to keep trying. A small detail, something said or found or overlooked, could suddenly open a door that would eventually lead to his wife's killer.

Ward slowly made his way to the kitchenette. He looked suspiciously at the mud-colored coffee left from the previous day. After starting a fresh pot, he went to the sliding glass door leading to the balcony and peered out.

During the night it had rained and temperatures dropped leaving a coating of ice on the patio furniture and metal railing. Two birds fluttered around an empty bird feeder at the far end of the balcony. He couldn't remember when he had last filled it. He moved back to the kitchen and watched coffee drip through the filter.

Keep busy; keep moving. He had followed that mantra throughout his life. Keep busy, keep moving and don't look back. But the past was all he had to hold onto now and it was slipping steadily away. His friends suggested it might be time to move on. But moving on meant he was leaving his beloved Barbara behind. Every step forward was a step away from her and that depressed him.

Ward showered, dressed and returned to the kitchen. He poured a cup of coffee, took a sip and moved to the couch. He then dialed Bull's number at the Standard Star newspaper office, leaving a message to meet him at ten at the City Deli. A part-time reporter, Bull was a freelance guru of all things electronic. His real name was Vincent Toolman and he had wanted to be a policeman, but couldn't pass the physical. Ditto for the military.

He had landed a job as a junior reporter covering local sporting events. Then he overheard the paper's editor talking about a detective living in New Rochelle who was creating quite a stir with his successful sleuthing. Vincent was twenty-four years old, five feet four inches, weighed about two hundred pounds and counting, and was almost completely bald. His sweet, chubby face reminded Ward of the Gerber baby.

They say the eyes are windows to the soul. From Ward's experience, knowing someone depended as much on the eyes doing the looking and judging as it did on the eyes being looked at. Those who didn't know Vincent saw only a short, fat guy waddling down the street and wrote him off as a loser. Granted he wasn't your Hollywood type, and granted his attempts at self-improvement changed as often as the weather, but in one respect he was turning out to be one hell of a detective. Vincent had suggested his own nickname—Bull. He said he felt macho with a nickname like that. In some ways the name fit. Once Vincent got his teeth into something, like a bulldog, he wouldn't let go. If Vincent couldn't find evidence, it probably didn't exist. After Barbara's death, Ward had come to rely on Bull to help him separate fact from fiction. As to him being macho, Ward left that for the ladies to decide.

The first time their paths crossed, Ward was reviewing his notes at the City Deli when his wristwatch alarm went off. The restaurant was empty except for a heavyset young man seated two tables over. The young man looked up as Ward's watch began beeping incessantly.

Ward could turn the alarm off temporarily, but couldn't disable it completely. The watch had been a gift from his wife, the last thing she'd given him. But Ward had little patience for ignorance, especially his own. He was fiddling with the buttons on his watch when the heavyset young man leaned in his direction and whispered, "Left button twice, hold it; right button twice."

"What?" Ward's eyes met Bull's.

"You want to turn it off permanently, right?" Bull held up the palm of one hand and mimicked pressing the buttons with the fingers of the other hand.

Ward's face reddened. "How was that again?"

"Press the left button twice and hold it. Then press the right button twice."

Ward pressed the buttons as instructed and the beeping stopped.

"You're Ward Emerson the private detective, aren't you?"

"Yes."

"I'm Vincent Toolman. I work for the Standard Star. They talk a lot about you there."

"Really? Anything you can repeat?"

"They say you're one of the best."

"I will definitely renew my subscription to your paper."

"You don't have a subscription. I checked." Bull's face broke into a huge grin.

Ward cleared some room at his table. "I'm impressed. Why don't you join me?"

Bull moved his coat, coffee, and half-eaten Danish to Ward's table. "That's one cool watch," Bull said with genuine enthusiasm as he forced his bulky body into a chair. "That's a Seiko Astron, isn't it? I've read about them. Even played with one at Macy's, but they're way out of my budget. It's the newest technology, a quartz watch. Japanese, right?"

"Yes, I think it's from Japan." Ward had regained his composure. "Was it the stupid look of desperation on my face that told you I didn't know how the damn thing worked?"

"Yeah."

They both laughed.

"How did you know who I was?" Ward asked.

"I've seen you in the editor's office a couple of times. I'm a reporter, but they only give me local stuff to cover, nothing exciting."

"Well, a lot of what I do is boring, too. It's not like the movies despite what my press agent says." Ward smiled and Bull matched his smile.

Bull suddenly became animated. His expansive body seemed to move in every direction as his tie rose and sank like a boat riding ocean swells. "I've been following your cases ever since you tracked down the kidnapper of that Mamaroneck kid. I've been wanting to meet you, but didn't have the nerve."

"Well, now's your chance." Ward lifted his coffee cup.

"They say you haven't been the same since your wife was murdered."

Ward froze.

"Crap, I'm sorry I said that. Sometimes I say stupid things." Bull began gathering his things to leave.

"No, that's okay." Ward forced a smile. He waved, indicating Bull should stay. "It's okay. Really." He took a sip of his coffee.

Bull shifted uneasily in his chair. "Teach me how to be a detective."

Ward choked, spilling coffee on the table. He grabbed a napkin and began wiping up the mess.

"Shit." Bull pulled napkins by the fistful from another dispenser and joined in.

When they finished, Ward leaned back in his chair. "Hold on now, my friend. Don't get me wrong. I appreciate your interest, but…"

"You need me," Bull interrupted as the big stupid smile reappeared, reminding Ward of a Labrador retriever he once owned.

"I need you? Well, now, Vincent. That's your name, isn't it?"

Bull nodded vigorously. "Yes, but my friends call me by my nickname, Bull."

"Well, Bull. That's a fresh approach, I'll confess. Why do I need you?" Ward narrowed his eyes, raised one eyebrow and stared at the young man. "I must have missed that part."

Bull's hands fluttered through the air like a flock of Canadian geese taking off from a marshy pond. "Today's criminals are moving to new technologies like computers and the only way to fight them is to out-tech them."

Ward put his cup down. "I'm listening."

"Beat them at their own game by using the latest tech stuff. I can help you do that. I know all about surveillance cameras and security systems, wire-tapping and neat stuff like that. I even built my own computer. It's primitive but it sort of works. Someday everyone will have their own computer."

Ward's interest grew. "Really?"

"Yes, and I can pick locks and jump-start cars, and," he nodded toward Ward's watch, "I can definitely teach you about your watch. All I ask is that you try me for a month. You don't have to buy equipment. I own most of the good stuff. And you don't have to pay me. Consider it an internship. I just know I can help you find your wife's murderer. If you don't think I can help you at the end of a month, I promise not to bother you again." If Vincent had a tail, it would have been wagging in eager anticipation.

Ward studied the young man. "Look, I'll be honest. I'm not safe. What I mean is that doing what I do isn't safe. It can be dangerous. You're a young man and you have your life ahead of you. Why would you want to jeopardize that?"

"I'll take that chance, if you'll let me." Bull's intense eyes focused hard on Ward. "To tell the truth, nothing much is happening in my life. I know I can make a contribution if I'm given a chance. I know I can."

There was something in what Vincent Toolman said that echoed feelings Ward had felt early in his own career. But the clincher was Bull's big, stupid grin. "Okay, one month."

That had been a year ago. Ward glanced back at the clock on his desk. There was still enough time to check phone messages before heading out to meet Bull at the deli.

Although Ward's first priority was finding Barbara's murderer, he could not shake Susan King's plea for help. He doubted she would find what she wanted on her own. Bull kept asking if he could help. Ward agreed but first wanted to establish Elizabeth's sanity.

He had called Jeff Keller at the precinct asking if there was anyone with contacts at Saint Michaels Hospital in Seawood, Long Island, anyone who could gain access to Elizabeth Dixon's medical records. Susan had said a nurse was with Elizabeth most of her time at Saint Michaels. Ward wanted to talk to that nurse.

Three messages were on his answering machine. Ward rewound the tape and played them back. The first message was from Jeff Keller. A friend of a friend who worked at Saint Michaels Hospital had discovered that Mildred Fancher was the nurse on duty when Elizabeth died. Jeff had put in a call and Mildred agreed to talk to Ward. Jeff cautioned Ward to be careful. The Feds were making it very difficult to go hunting in medical files.

The second message was from Mildred Fancher. She was deliberately vague and brief, leaving only her telephone number and when she could be reached at home.

The third message was an encouraging message from Bull. Ward had asked him to check up on one of the Brooklyn mafia families, the Gerberti family. Bull finished his message by describing his news as possibly "blazing!" Ward smiled. Bull was constantly working to stay "linguistically hip" as he put it. Periodically he would try out new slang just to see how it felt and how Ward reacted. If Ward protested or raised one of his eyebrows, Bull added it to his treasure chest of favorite expressions. Secretly, Ward knew Bull just wanted to drive him nuts.

Ward grabbed his coat, but before leaving he went onto the balcony, scooped up sunflower seeds and tossed them onto the patio table. As he slid the balcony door closed, two birds had already descended on the seeds. Ward smiled. Barbara would have been pleased.

Chapter 7: Finding Patterns

Although Ward escaped from the world's problems at Two Toms Tavern, he did his best thinking at City Deli on Main Street, New Rochelle. Weekdays it was his office, on Sundays a sanctuary where he and Barbara would reconnect after a hectic workweek. Sitting for hours by their favorite window, they would share a lunch, read the *Times* or *The New Yorker* and talk. Barbara had taught Ward the fine art of the three-hour lunch. He discovered that the test of a real soul mate was that you never tired spending time together.

After Barbara died, Ward avoided the City Deli. Then one day he just walked in and sat down at their table. He took a deep breath, and a sense of peace told him he had come home. Henry, the owner, a tall Ukrainian from Kiev who treated regulars as family, brought Ward his usual coffee and pastry. "On the house!" Henry briefly touched Ward's shoulder as if to say it's going to be all right and went about his business.

When Ward arrived at the restaurant for his meeting with Bull, the morning commuters had already grabbed their coffees and bagged lunches, leaving the restaurant nearly empty. Ward went straight to the public phone and dialed Susan at her work number. She picked up on the second ring.

"It's Ward Emerson. I need some information on your family. Is this a good time to talk?"

"Wait a minute while I close my door." While she was away, Ward pulled a pencil and notepad from his coat pocket.

"Okay, I'm back."

"What does your Uncle Paul do for a living?"

"He was the captain of our family fishing boat, the Sea Angel, but he's retired. His son runs the boat now."

"A commercial boat?"

"No, a pleasure fishing boat. He takes people fishing along Long Island and the Jersey shore."

"How many siblings did Elizabeth have?"

"Four: Paul is the youngest, then the twins, Edward and Albert, and Pete. Uncle Paul is the only one still living. Elizabeth was the oldest."

"Have they always lived in Seawood?"

"No, they were all born in lower Manhattan but moved to Seawood after grandfather developed lung problems. They felt living by the sea would help his condition."

"How old was Elizabeth when the family left the city?"

"Is this important?"

"It could be."

"What was your question?"

"How old was Elizabeth when she left the city?"

"In her late teens, I think. My mother would know all those details."

"What was Elizabeth's husband's name?"

"Todd. His name was Todd."

"What can you tell me about him?"

"I really don't know much. Elizabeth and Todd met on Long Island and from what Elizabeth told me, I think they had a good marriage. Todd became captain of the family boat. But he had a bad heart. Elizabeth told me he took the boat out one day and was headed back when a fire broke out in the engine room. The boat nearly sank, but Todd was able to get it back to the dock. That night he suffered a heart attack and died on the way to the hospital."

"How old was your mother when that happened?"

"Mother wasn't born yet. Elizabeth was eight months pregnant when Todd died so she was on her own. She said those were the dark years when so many family members died."

"And you said Paul is the only remaining brother?"

"That's right. All of her other brothers are buried in the Dwyer plot."

"And you said Elizabeth did not discuss with you where her final resting place should be before she was taken to the hospital for the last time. Is that right?"

"Yes."

"Susan, this information is helpful. Call me if you need me or if you think of anything else."

"I will. And Ward, thank you."

Ward hung up and returned to his table. He was just finishing his first cup of coffee when Bull arrived.

"What's hanging?" Bull had lectured Ward on the importance for young men to keep up with fashion trends. Unfortunately, his choice of clothes sometimes raised questions and eyebrows. Today he wore a red nylon jacket that was too tight across the middle and too short. His blue bell-bottom pants occasionally revealed a pair of black and white sneakers. Over his shoulder, he carried a fringed, crescent-shaped, soft leather bag that reminded Ward of a pony express saddlebag he had seen in a museum. The thought of Bull galloping up the Post Road delivering mail in his hip outfit brought a smile to Ward's face.

Bull pointed to his clothes. "Do I look like a dude who's with it?"

"Absolutely," Ward said enthusiastically, the word almost catching in his throat.

Henry came over and took Bull's order.

"I'll try the chicken pot pie, a hot pastrami sandwich and a glass of milk."

Ward gave his partner a questioning look, but Bull just smiled at him with his dopey grin. Bull removed a notepad from his bag and began flipping through its pages. "I met your friends, agents Taylor and Sakes at the FBI field office in the city. They called and said they had something I should give you. They wanted to know how you were doing and why you haven't dropped by lately. I told them you would call. They asked if you still felt the Gerberti family was the prime suspect in your wife's murder. I told them you valued their opinions on this."

"And what did they say?"

"I'm getting to that." Bull glanced at his notepad. "I told them you believed the Gerberti family had your wife murdered as possible payback because you spoiled their drug operations. Your friends mentioned two families, the Gerberti family out of Brooklyn and the Ramirez family from Jersey. Since both families were into drug trafficking, they both had a motive for wanting to get back at you. But none of your friends at the office felt either family would have taken the risk what with the Feds putting so much pressure on their operations. Murdering your wife would draw too much heat.

"Agents Taylor and Sakes both felt it has to be someone else, but who that someone else might be remains a mystery."

Ward stared long and hard at Bull. "No, the Ramirez family is small potatoes. And my investigations were targeting the Gerberti operations in Westchester, not the Ramirez family. If the Gerberti family was not involved in Barbara's murder, we're back to square one with nothing to go on and no direction to take. I don't like it. Until we prove otherwise, the Gerberti stay at the top of our list of suspects, understand?"

Bull started to respond but instead flipped to a new section of his notepad. "You know that case you were working on, the stolen paintings from the Boston Museum?"

Ward nodded. "What about it?"

"I called the museum director. He said it definitely was a professional heist. The thieves knew how to get past security and, as you predicted, one of the paintings turned up on the black-market in Europe. They believe an international ring is probably behind the heist with a local family assisting for a piece of the action."

Henry arrived with Bull's food. Grabbing half the pastrami sandwich, Bull began devouring it until he caught Ward's disapproving gaze.

Ward shook his head. "Too much pastrami is not good for you. I thought you were trying to lose weight?"

With both cheeks stuffed, Bull looked like a chipmunk. "I'm a growing boy."

Ward smiled. "That's the problem. You're growing in all directions. I believe just last week you said something about wanting to slim down?"

Bull paused for a moment. "Yeah, but one pastrami sandwich isn't bad. Besides, I ordered the chicken potpie because everyone knows chicken is good for you. It's a scientific fact! Everyone knows that." Bull picked up his fork and began digging into the chicken dish.

Ward feigned a look of surprise. "You're right, come to think of it. I seem to remember reading a scientific paper on that very topic when I was at Princeton. I think the title was *Chicken is Good for You. It's a Scientific Fact!*"

Bull ignored Ward and took another forkful.

Ward moved on. "By the way, did you get to meet agent Brennan?"

"Yeah, but first I met a couple of blazing chicks while I waited downstairs for the elevator. The girls work for NY Telephone on the fifth floor. There are lots of really good-looking girls in that building. If you hang around the lobby, you can connect."

Ward nodded. "I see. So when you did manage to break yourself loose from all those blazing women and made it to the sixth floor, what did Brennan say?"

Bull reached into his bag, pulled out a large envelope and handed it to Ward. "She asked me to give this to you."

Ward removed three reports from the envelope, read Brennan's attached note, and then scanned the documents.

Bull watched Ward flip back and forth through the pages. A woman's photo was attached to the right-hand corner of each report. Bull took another forkful of chicken, then leaned over and peered at the photos. He put his fork down as he stared at the bloodied images in the photos. "Who are these women?"

"These women were murdered in the same ritualistic way Barbara was killed."

Ward handed the reports to Bull and finished his coffee while Bull looked over the documents.

"What are we looking for?" Bull asked as he studied the profiles of the victims.

"Patterns, data, facts. Anything that points back to whomever killed these women."

"So you think these victims were murdered by the same person?"

Ward nodded. "Well, we know they were killed in the same weird way. Now we need to see if there are any similarities in their profiles. The things these women have in common would suggest there is a pattern and a possible link between them. That link may help us figure out what drew the murderer to them."

"A pattern?"

"Yes, look for patterns."

Bull looked over the profiles again. "Let's see. All three women were in their twenties or early thirties. All were murdered in the same way. But they were murdered in different cities and years apart. This is weird. If we're looking for a serial killer, he seems to go long periods without committing another murder. That's not the way serial killers usually operate, is it?"

"Not all serial killers fit the general pattern. There are exceptions. Our killer may be committing murders somewhere outside the country and no one has connected the dots. Differences, if looked at from another angle, can become similarities. Different cities suggest the guy travels and the cities he visits may tell us something about why he chooses these cities. Where the victim was murdered in the city may point us to another pattern. Look closely at the pictures of the women. Do you see anything else? Try to look beyond the blood. Try to see what these women looked like before they were murdered. All are quite beautiful, don't you agree?"

Bull studied the photos more closely. "Well, yes. Yes, they are."

Ward flipped through the photos again. "Unless the murderer knew these women, there was something about them, something that attracted our murderer to them and not to other women. They all have some physical features that are similar. All have long hair, white skin, and straight noses. From their descriptions we know they were slender. These qualities may have attracted our killer. My hunch is that these women were chosen for very specific reasons. Our job is to find the reasons and let these patterns lead the way. Let's start researching their backgrounds." Ward put the reports back in the envelope. "In the meantime, you asked to help with the Susan King inquiry, so I have an assignment with that case."

Bull wiped mustard from his lips as he finished his sandwich. "Okay, now we're talking. That chick, Susan King, was blazing, don't you think?"

Ward smiled. "Yes, she was blazing, but stay focused on what I need you to do. Find out all you can about their family fishing boat, the Sea Angel. It's moored at Seawood, Long Island. And check on the Dwyer family. Find out what people in the area think about them, but don't be obvious. Tell people you're writing an article for your paper on fishing off of Long Island. We don't want the family to get nervous and go after Susan. Here are a few names to get you started. Check the newspapers; go back as far as the early twenties."

Bull whistled. "Prehistoric times? Did they have newspapers then?"

Ward smiled "No, smart ass. They wrote on stone tablets which they carried in their animal-skin, bell-bottom pants' pockets"

They both laughed.

"What are we looking for?" Before Ward could answer, Bull answered his own question. "I know, we're looking for patterns!"

"Right, but let's give it a shot. Something about that gravesite terrified Elizabeth. We have to find out what it was. So while you check out the Sea Angel, I have a date at the cemetery."

Peter Saunders

Chapter 8: The Guest

Traffic was unusually light on 95 as Ward headed for the cemetery on Long Island the next morning. At the Throgs Neck Expressway, traffic slowed to a crawl. Beating traffic was a major pastime for New Yorkers, and a topic of conversation at just about any party. Boasting rights were yours if by some miracle you discovered a way to beat the long lines of cars and trucks. Ward would not be boasting today. His car inched along the Southern State Parkway for half an hour till he passed a fender-bender on the side of the road. The drivers stood arguing while a policewoman sat in her cruiser writing her report. Thirty minutes later Ward pulled into Holy Ghost Cemetery.

Winds off the Atlantic had picked up causing the rain, now heavy, to fall at sharp angles making visibility difficult. Ward slowed, switched the windshield wipers to high, drove past the cemetery office, and pulled up beside a locator sign at a crossroads. The avenues were clearly marked, but the numbers weren't in sequence. Ward glanced at Susan's note. The family plot number was listed but not the avenue it was on. He drove back to the main office, hurried up the steps and went in.

As he stood in the foyer shaking rain from his trench coat, Ward noticed to his left a large waiting room. The stone fireplace at one end looked inviting. Across from the foyer behind a glass partition were rows of metal storage shelves containing record boxes. A circular staircase stood to one side of the shelves, suggesting more boxes were stored upstairs. A sign on the wall pointed down the hall to a counter and a welcome sign.

As Ward approached the desk, a woman poked her head out from a back room. "Oh, I thought I heard someone come in. I'll be right out."

Ward removed his coat and hung it on a coat rack in the corner. While he waited, he studied an old print on the wall depicting the cemetery in the early eighteen hundreds surrounded by farms.

Soon the woman emerged from the backroom. "I'm Gloria Zoroya. May I help you?" Gloria wore a brown woolen cardigan over a cream-colored blouse, a brown-plaid skirt, and dark shoes with dark stockings. Her reading glasses hung from a silver chain around her neck. She reminded Ward of his first grade teacher. She had a kind face and looked genuinely pleased to see him.

"I've come to pay my respects to Elizabeth Dwyer Dixon, a friend."

Gloria glanced out the window behind her. "Dear, the weather is not cooperating for a gravesite visit, is it? Have you come far?"

"I drove in from New Rochelle."

"Did traffic at the bridge hold you up?"

"No, the bridge was fine. I passed one accident, but otherwise the trip was good." Ward pulled out the paper Susan had given him and handed it to Gloria. "I'm having trouble finding the right avenue and the family plot."

She glanced at the paper. "Yes, I understand. Our numbering system is quite antiquated. Dwyer Dixon did you say?"

"Yes, she is buried in the Dwyer family plot."

"That name does ring a bell. Mrs. Dixon's burial was quite recent, wasn't it?"

"Yes."

"I'll get our master records book for that name. Why don't you sit by the fireplace in our waiting room? I'll meet you there."

Ward retreated to the waiting room and stood enjoying the fireplace's welcoming glow. The room was a bit smoky, but the warmth was a relief from the damp chill. Stained glass windows above the mantel cast a soft and peaceful hue throughout the darkened room. The last time Ward had been at a cemetery was to bury Barbara. It had rained the day of her burial and after the funeral Ward returned and stood alone by the gravesite until he was informed they were closing the cemetery.

The sound of footsteps descending the metal stairs across the hall drew Ward back to the present. Gloria returned with an enormous leather book. The faded letters DWR were stamped in gold on its binding. She placed the book in the middle of the oval table that stood in front of the fireplace and opened to the first section. "This is the oldest of our records."

Gallery of the Chosen

Ward looked over her shoulder as she put on her glasses and turned the yellowed pages. Each page was divided into four columns labeled across the top: date of burial, name of the deceased, plot number and cause of death. Many of the "cause of death" sections were blank.

"Let's see, Elizabeth Dwyer Dixon. You said it was the Dwyer family plot?"

"Yes."

Gloria quickly flipped the pages. "Dwyer, Dwyer. We have several families with that name. Do you have any other information such as the exact date of burial? We know it was relatively recent."

"No, I don't know the exact date."

Gloria glanced up and studied him for a moment. "That's quite all right. You have the plot number and the year, so we'll find her." She turned back to the book. "Perhaps if you look over some of the other family names you will recognize the right one." Gloria stoked the fire while Ward scanned the pages.

Pulling out his notepad, he looked up the names of Susan's other relatives. On page twenty-four he found the correct Dwyer family. The office records indicated that Elizabeth was the eighth person buried there. Ward looked at the names again on his notepad and those on the ledger. According to the ledger, 'a guest' was buried in the family plot.

"I think I found the right entry, but it says there were seven people buried here before Elizabeth. She should have been the seventh; not the eighth."

Gloria hurried to his side. "Where?"

"Here" He pointed to the word 'guest' in the ledger. "I'm confused by this entry. Could this be an error?"

"Well, now you have me in a difficult spot." Gloria glanced at the guest's burial date—1948. I must confess that our record keeping before the 1960s was somewhat chaotic. We've always kept three types of records—a master record book, an internment book and a plot book. Unfortunately some of the information contained in one book may not have been transferred to the other ledgers. After 1955 a standard system was begun but to tell the truth, progress has been slow at best. Of course, there have been rare occasions when a name was put under the wrong family name, but, as I said, to our knowledge that seldom happened."

Gloria looked at the names on Ward's notepad. "This certainly seems to be the right Dwyer family. But perhaps someone in the family failed to note that permission was given for a guest to be buried with the family."

Ward looked at Gloria. "A what?"

"A guest of the family. It was not uncommon for families at that time to bury members from a previous marriage, or even a friend."

"Really? I thought the best thing about guests was that they had to leave at some point?"

Gloria ignored Ward's comment. "Oh, no, it was quite common for families to use plots for a number of different purposes. During the Depression, some families sold gravesites and some even gave space to those who couldn't afford a grave."

"But didn't they have to record who the guest was? A name has to be recorded somewhere."

Gloria removed her glasses and cleared her throat. "Yes, it is odd that a name was not recorded. There is the possibility that the family planned to bury a friend or guest but never did. So whoever the guest was may never have been buried. That would explain the absence of an actual name. Let me check the internment and plot records. This will take a few minutes." She went back into the records room and climbed the stairs.

While she was gone, Ward rechecked the listings for the Dwyer family members. The grandparents both died of natural causes. Pete died from drowning in 1937. Next to Todd, Elizabeth husband, was the date 1937 and the comment "Died from heart attack." Brother Edward died in 1938. No cause of death was recorded. Brother Al died in 1955 from tuberculosis. No date or cause of death was recorded for the mysterious guest. Ward remembered Susan's comment that Elizabeth felt those years were the dark years when so many members of her family died.

Gloria returned with two other books. "Let's start with the internment records." She flipped to the correct family plots. "Let's see, yes. Here it is. It does indicate a guest was buried and it identifies the guest as J. Lynks." Gloria pushed the book closer to Ward.

The comment "family friend" was recorded. For cause of death, "cause unknown" was written.

"Was it unusual to list 'cause unknown' for someone's death?"

"No, not unusual at all. Medical knowledge then was not what it is today. If they didn't know the cause for the individual's death, and unless there was some particular reason for finding out, it was not uncommon to describe the cause as unknown. Of course you could check the death certificate. We don't keep copies of those. The Suffolk County Courthouse would have a copy of the death certificate." Gloria opened the final records book, but could find no mention of a J. Lynks.

"Strange, the name J. Lynks does not appear in this record book. She closed the book. "As I have said, there is a good possibility that although one record indicates who the guest might have been, because there is no supporting entry in our other records, short of opening the grave, we have no way of knowing if the guest, who appears to be J. Lynks, is actually buried there." Gloria lowered her glasses, leaned closer and asked in a half whisper, "Is anything wrong?"

"No, I was just curious."

"I'm afraid I've not been much of a help."

Ward collected his coat and hat, and turned toward Gloria. "Nonsense, you have been very helpful."

"Oh, just a moment." Gloria went back to her office then returned handing him a map. "I've highlighted the route to Mrs. Dixon's grave site."

"Thank you." He shook her hand and left.

Ward could see Gloria standing on the porch watching as he drove away. A few minutes later he stood before a large, marble headstone with the word Dwyer inscribed across the top. The names of all the family members were there, just as Susan had said but no indication a guest had joined them. Ward said a short prayer and headed back to New Rochelle. If a mysterious guest was indeed buried with the family, Ward suspected the guest, J. Lynks, was somehow connected to Elizabeth's last request. Now he had to prove it.

Peter Saunders

Chapter 9: The Threat

Physical abuse was something Ward could not tolerate. Therefore, when Bull presented him with a plea to find a woman's husband, a stock analyst who had run off with a college cheerleader leaving his wife with major bruises on her body and three kids to raise on food stamps and church handouts, Ward didn't hesitate. A week later, he had tracked Mr. Tough Guy to North White Plains and shot a photo of him at the door of his secret hideaway giving his cheerleader a kiss. Bull would deliver the photo and street address to the wife's lawyer and police. Having done a good day's work, Ward headed home.

The old apartment where Ward lived had seen better days—much better days. Located two blocks from Main Street in New Rochelle, the building had long ago lost whatever charms it once claimed. Ward lived on the seventh floor. There was an elevator that rarely worked and a superintendent who worked even less.

Some weeks had passed since Ward's visit to the Holy Ghost Cemetery. There were no new developments in either his search for his wife's murderer or in finding why Elizabeth Dixon was terrified of being buried in the family plot.

This evening Ward slowly climbed the stairs to his apartment. It was too late to run into Rachel Hughes, the shapely widow across the hall who decided to pull Ward's life together. She had sympathetic eyes and a heart that matched. Barbara had organized Ward's social life. After her murder, Ward faded into the woodwork, losing track of his neighbors and the local gossip.

Once a week Rachel brought over a plate of food. Sometimes it was a whole dinner, sometimes only dessert. Sitting together on Ward's balcony, Rachel would tell him about her wild daughter who was into a second husband. On occasion, if Ward were out, Rachel would put the food in containers, placing them in a plastic bag she hung from his apartment's doorknob. Maybe Ward should have refused her offerings, but he still wasn't eating regular meals, so he accepted them. Besides, he enjoyed her company.

There was no bag hanging from the doorknob this evening. Once inside his apartment, he threw his jacket on the couch, ignoring the blinking light on the answering machine. He poured himself a stiff scotch, walked onto his small balcony and collapsed in a lounge chair. Stillness clung to the trees and streets below. The Embassy theatre on Main Street had finished its eight o'clock movie and the exodus of the few patrons who still visited the old theatre had begun. Engines started up and then died away into the distance.

Barbara and Ward loved the sad movie house with its ornate, frescoed walls and empty balconies. An enormous, ancient organ covered with dust and cobwebs sat forgotten in the shadowy center of the upper balcony. The enclosed mall out in the suburbs had robbed the Embassy and most downtown stores of any real business. Trying to lure customers back, the theatre owners offered double features, but no one seemed to notice. Even the manager had given up and only occasionally showed up, sitting in the last row drinking liquor from a paper bag. Ward and Barbara didn't care. They adopted the old movie house as their very own and went often. Strange, but that seemed so long ago, Ward thought, staring at his empty glass.

He took a deep breath and closed his eyes. Muffled voices from another apartment balcony drifted into his consciousness, then faded.

The insistent ringing of his telephone broke his peaceful moment. He made it to the telephone just as Susan King was leaving a message.

"I'm here, Susan."

"Sorry to call so late, but I'm very upset. I'm being accused of disgracing the family and Uncle Paul is threatening me." There was panic in her voice.

"What's happening?"

"I called my mother and told her about our meeting. I thought maybe I could convince her to talk to you, but she became very angry. She said Elizabeth was delirious, and I had to accept that. She screamed something about grandmother never allowing anyone to embarrass the family like this. Private detectives were the scum of the earth and routinely blackmail families with stuff they make up. That's what she said."

"Really?" Ward feigned surprise but knew detectives who matched that description. He could hear Susan struggling to control herself and waited till she calmed down.

"Uncle Paul can be emotional, but I didn't expect him to scream and threaten me. I'm his godchild. He phoned right after my mother hung up and said if I didn't cut off all communications with you immediately, he would get a lawyer to stop me."

"Stop you from what?"

"Hiring you, I guess."

"There is no law against talking to a detective," Ward pointed out.

"My uncle is a powerful man in the Seawood community. I've no idea what he can and cannot do."

Ward thought the family's reaction to Susan's news was predictable but seemed excessive. Even if Uncle Paul was a hothead, his threats suggested there might be something he didn't want uncovered. On the other hand, if he was really willing to involve the law, he probably didn't have too much to hide. And Susan's grandmother might have been delirious despite what Susan believed. The family might be trying to protect everyone from those low life detectives her mother referred to.

"Did you find anything?"

"Find anything?" Susan's question caught Ward off guard.

"About my grandmother and her request?"

"No, nothing yet. But there is a risk that if you continue, your relatives' anger will only increase. Your uncle may try to get the courts to stop you."

"Can he do that?"

"He can try."

"But I'm not doing anything wrong, am I?" Susan asked.

"Well, from our perspective no; from their perspective, plenty. My snooping around could be seen as discrediting the good reputation of your family. They might be able to make it very difficult for us. And there is one other thing, far more important that you need to consider."

"What's that?"

"It's possible the truth behind your grandmother's request could bring a lot of pain to your family. You have to decide if your grandmother would have wanted that."

Susan said nothing. One of the lousiest parts of Ward's job was pulling back the curtain of deception, revealing the secrets of a loved one's life. Usually the secret was hidden in the shadows of a family's consciousness like a love affair or a dark compulsion. Sometimes it was something out in the light that all but those directly involved could see. Ward knew how self-deception could grow on individuals. Showing clients the dark web of lies in their families caused the most pain. So whenever he could, he left the curtains drawn. When pushed, he showed his clients how to pull the curtain back and left the rest to them. The old paradox of human nature wanting the truth uncovered and then covered again, kept him employed.

Some families found it in their hearts to forgive their loved ones and buried the truth forever. There were those, however, who took sport in raging against the past and enjoyed dragging their family's dark secrets again and again into the light as punishment. "I'm like a gravedigger," Ward complained to Barbara one evening. "I'm digging up the secrets of the dead. I hear their confessions and say 'sleep well,' but I know some poor souls will never be put to rest, and no good will come from the revelations brought to light."

"Susan, why don't you let sleeping dogs lie?" he suggested.

"What do you mean?" Ward could hear the sound of defeat creeping into her voice.

"I mean, why don't you let go of this?"

"I can't. I can't do that."

Ward tried another tack. "You said your mother and uncle thought your grandmother was delirious when she made her request."

"That's what they said."

"And they heard your grandmother make her request?"

"Yes."

"Did anyone else hear it? A nurse or doctor?"

"Yes, our family doctor, Dr. Bell was there. And a hospital nurse." Susan's tone suddenly went icy. "What are you suggesting?"

"I believe your grandmother's request was genuine. Please remember I am trying to help you here, but we need to prove that Elizabeth was not delirious. If she was rational then we have to ask why your family insists Elizabeth was not. I need to establish Elizabeth's state of mind from someone other than a family member if I am to go forward. How long has Dr. Bell been your family doctor?"

"It seems forever. Maybe thirty years. He goes way back."

"Did Dr. Bell agree with your mother and uncle that Elizabeth was delirious?"

There was a long, hollow silence at the other end of the line. Ward figured Susan knew where he was heading. He waited for her response.

"He agreed with them. He called a week after Elizabeth died and told me how sorry he was for the family loss. He tried to cheer me up, but when I mentioned my grandmother's request and insisted she was not delirious, he cut me off. He said he did not want to discuss it and he suggested I was overreacting. He offered to prescribe a relaxant. When I tried to argue with him, he hung up."

"Can you think of any reason why Dr. Bell would say that about your grandmother if he knew it was a lie? Any reason at all?"

"No. I have gone over this a hundred times; I don't know why he would side with my mother and uncle."

"Is it possible they are right, no matter how painful it may be to accept? Does it not seem reasonable that under the stress of impending death, Elizabeth's imagined fears could have been exaggerated?"

"Elizabeth knew who we were and called us by our names. She was very frightened, but she was not delirious. I believe my grandmother was trying to tell me something painful she needed to deal with before she died."

"So, you're saying you believe your grandmother had a secret?"

"Yes."

"Given what you've said and the way your family has reacted are you sure you want to know that secret? As I say, isn't it better just to leave things as they are?"

"Believe me, a part of me wants to drop this, but my heart tells me my grandmother had another reason for making her request."

"Another reason?"

"I believe my grandmother could not bring herself to tell me her secret, but she wants me to find out what it is."

"And why would she want you to do that?"

"Something strange my grandmother said to me before she died made me feel this way."

"Go on."

"When my mother and uncle stepped out of the room, Elizabeth kept saying she was sorry. She begged me to forgive her and to help her. She wouldn't tell me why she needed to be forgiven. At first when she asked me to help her I thought she was referring to her wish to be buried in a separate plot. Now I think she was asking me to help her win her forgiveness. I'm not sure how I'm to do this, but I am sure it's tied to that gravesite. Does any of this make sense?"

"Yes. So you feel knowing Elizabeth's secret and why she did not want to be buried in the family plot may help her win forgiveness?"

"Yes."

"And you will be comfortable with me knowing her secret?"

"Mr. Emerson, you're the only hope I have. I trust you."

Ward took a deep breath. He told Susan he would get back to her in a week or so. He promised to do his best, and then he asked for the telephone numbers and addresses of her relatives.

"Susan, try to relax. Try to forget about all of this until I contact you. When your mother and uncle calm down, they'll come around, but until I get back to you, don't discuss this further with your relatives. Stall them if you have to. Tell them you are thinking over what they said. That may satisfy them until I finish my preliminary digging. Can you do this?"

"Yes, yes, I think so."

Ward was about to hang up when Susan hit him with a question of her own.

"Ward, that stuff my mother said about detectives, about them making up lies and blackmailing their clients, that's not true about you, is it?"

"No, Susan, that's not true about me."

Chapter 10: The Switch

Ward sat in his living room reviewing his notes on the Elizabeth Dwyer Dixon case. The sun had just peeked over the old colonial houses across the street, bathing his balcony in brilliant morning sunshine. His sleep had been restless and filled with fragments of disturbing dreams. The dreams were not about his wife's murder; they were about Elizabeth and her fears. In the dream, Ward stood at the Dwyer family gravesite saying a brief prayer. It was late afternoon. A chilling wind swept across the rows of granite gravestones. Ward shivered. As he ended his prayer, he suddenly felt the presence of someone behind him. He turned, but there was no one there. Still, he could not shake the feeling that someone had been standing behind him. With that, the dream ended and Ward woke up.

He went into the kitchen, poured a cup of coffee and returned to his chair. After his conversation with Susan, he knew he could not drop her case; he wanted to see it through. Then his telephone rang. It was Bull.

"I've got some stuff on the Dwyer family. I'll be there in thirty minutes."

The discovery of the mysterious J. Lynks buried in the Dwyer plot suggested Susan's grandmother probably knew she would have an unwanted guest beside her. But there was still the nagging question of just how clear Elizabeth's mind was on the day she begged to be buried elsewhere.

Ward glanced at his watch. At 9 a.m., as instructed, he dialed Mildred Fancher, the nurse who tended to Elizabeth during her final hours.

"Hello, Mildred Fancher? This is Ward Emerson calling."

"Yes, I was expecting your call."

"I appreciate you helping me out. A member of Elizabeth's family contacted me. I am trying to...."

Mildred cut him off. "If this could lead to a lawsuit against the hospital, I can't help you. I have to protect my job." Mildred's voice quavered slightly.

"No, no. This has nothing to do with the hospital. Elizabeth Dixon made some personal requests before she died. I just want to know what mental state she was in at the time."

"Well, I don't want to be dragged into any family lawsuit either."

"I assure you that whatever you tell me will be kept confidential. You have my word."

There was a long pause on the other end. "Okay then. I don't mind helping if I can, but I can't be dragged into anything illegal. I wouldn't be doing this if Jeff Keller hadn't spoken so highly of you. My father was a policeman, so I try to help when I can."

"I understand. Anything you can tell me about Mrs. Dixon will be greatly appreciated."

"I was on duty the day she died and was with the family right up to Elizabeth Dixon's final moments. She was upset about something, but her granddaughter—I've forgotten her name."

"Susan."

"Yes. Susan seemed to have a calming effect on her."

"Was Mrs. Dixon sedated?"

"No, no. She refused medications. She recognized her family and talked briefly to them and to the doctor and her priest."

"So would you say her mind was clear?"

"Yes, she knew she was dying, but she was upset about something—funeral arrangements, I think. The family left the room and went down the hall to discuss whatever it was that was upsetting her and returned shortly. They seemed to have resolved the issue because Susan told her grandmother everything would be all right. That calmed Mrs. Dixon and a few hours later she slipped into a coma and died peacefully. That's all I know."

Ward thanked Mildred and hung up. That was one for Susan and zero for Mother Angela and Uncle Paul.

The pounding on Ward's apartment door signaled Bull had arrived. He burst in waving a folder under Ward's nose. "I've got some weird stuff on the Dwyer family." The excitement in Bull's voice told Ward he would like what Bull had found.

"How good is this stuff? Is it worth a free lunch?" Ward laughed as he led the way into the living room. Bull tossed his coat on the couch, made his way to the coffee table, and began spreading out photocopied articles.

"Boss, what I have may be worth a year's supply of lunches." Bull pulled a candy bar from his pocket and opened its wrapper.

Ward laughed. "You sound pretty confident. So what do you have?"

Bull pulled two news articles from the pile of photocopies and pointed at the headlines. One read, "Town Council to Consider Applications for Docking Privileges" and the other read, "Town Council Denies Docking Rights." The headlines were about Seawood's Town Council and docking privileges at its piers. Bull searched for another article while Ward scanned the copies.

"Here it is." Bull handed Ward another article. "Local Fishing Family Loses Appeal." "Looks like Susan's family might have been into more than fishing. The Dwyers were rubbing elbows with some pretty powerful mafia members in that area, both the Gerberti and Agrelo families show up in my research."

Ward's head snapped up. "The Gerberti! Are you sure?"

Bull nodded. "Yep, there were some strange goings-on out Seawood way." Bull pointed to another news headline: "Town Council Calls Special Session."

Bull took a bite of his candy bar and continued. "I discovered the Dwyer family was one of the earliest families to start a fishing business at Seawood. They had a prime location at the pier that dates back to the 1930s. Locals told me that half the town's kids had summer jobs working on the Dwyer boat. But then, out of the blue, the council voted to take away their docking space."

"Why?"

"Well, those few who could remember and were willing to talk, told me the arrangement for docking privileges between boat owners and Seawood's Council had been pretty informal up until then. It was a gentleman's agreement sort of thing. Then the Council decided it would formalize the leasing of docking spaces at its piers and all interested parties should apply in writing. No big deal, except when the Council met again to award the docking spaces, the Dwyer family was told their application had been denied, and they had sixty days to move their boat and take their business elsewhere. The minutes from the meeting stated that the Dwyer's boat didn't meet safety regulations."

Ward shook his head. "Sounds like a pretty weak argument."

"Exactly what I thought. So the Dwyer's hired a lawyer and appealed the decision, but that didn't sway the Council. They awarded their dock space to a company…," Bull thumbed through his handwritten notes taken from the transcripts. "Here it is! The dock space was awarded to Old World Charter Cruises owned by the Agrelo family—to run sunset cruises and nighttime fishing trips."

Ward's eyebrows arched upward as he gave a low whistle. "Antonio Agrelo? The liquor and gambling baron?"

Bull smiled. "None other than the chief rival of the Gerberti family. From what I can make out, around 1925 a racetrack was built in Brooklyn. Customers from the track soon discovered that two competing firms, the Old World Cruises and Sea Wolf Enterprises were running boats out of a nearby pier for one and all interested in fishing and some friendly evening gambling."

"Let me guess. None of the customers caught fish?"

Bull smiled. "For the record, everyone caught the limit, but hold on, I'm getting to that. I'm told some boats carried fewer poles than there were customers and still everyone caught fish. One guy who had worked on the boats as a teenager tells me their freezers were filled with frozen fish which were handed to customers as the boats approached the docks."

Ward laughed. "Just to make things look good, no doubt. Quite a sight, customers loaded with booze staggering off the boats in business suits."

Bull nodded. "Yeah, they would step off the boat carrying frozen fish under their arms and empty wallets in their pockets."

Ward stood up. "I'm getting orange juice. Want anything from the kitchen?"

"No, I'm on a diet."

Ward froze in his tracks. "Really? What about that candy bar?"

Bull leaned back and locked his fingers behind his head. "I'm going cold turkey from this minute on."

"Bull, I'm proud of you, if you mean what you say."

Bull pointed to the remaining candy bar on the table. "See this candy bar?"

Ward nodded. "I see it."

"I'll bet you it's still here at the end of today's meeting."

Ward smiled. "What do you want to bet?"

Bull thought for a moment. "Well, if it isn't here, then I'll buy you lunch next time we're at the diner."

"Lunch?"

Bull scratched his head. "You're right. Buying lunch when I am on a diet doesn't make sense, does it? How about coffee and dessert?"

"How about coffee?"

Bull eyed the candy bar. "Deal. If this candy bar is still here when our meeting is over, you buy the coffee."

"You're on."

Bull eyed the tempting candy bar but kept his hands tightly locked behind his head.

"So the mafia families are doing illegal gambling off shore near Rockaway?" Ward picked up where they had left off.

"Yep. Everyone's happy, except that an ambitious reporter writes an article suggesting that the police should check out local fishing businesses after some unlucky guy with bullet holes in the back of his skull and a bunch of IOU's in his pocket washes up on Coney Island. The Agrelo and Gerberti families begin looking for alternative docks further out on the Long Island. Seawood meets all their requirements. It's only twenty minutes from the racetrack and was still a sleepy little fishing village with rotting piers and only a few fishing boats, like the Dwyers, doing business. One guy said they couldn't give dock space away. It was a perfect spot."

Ward nodded. "So the families decided to move their operations to Seawood and convinced the town to give them the Dwyer's docking space. But that would mean it's game over for the Dwyer business." Ward paused, looked at the articles again and then continued. "I'm a little lost here. Susan told me their family fishing boat still runs out of Seawood. But you say their docking space was taken away from them. Is that right?"

Bull raised his eyebrows, closed his eyes and tilted his head to one side pretending he was deep in thought as he weighed Ward's question. "Yes and no."

"Yes and no? What the hell does that mean?"

Bull slapped the table with such force that the candy bar bounced onto the floor. In a flash Bull scooped it up.

"The Town Council tells the Dwyer family their space has been given to someone else. As I said, the Dwyers' appeal but as you can see from the headline the appeal was denied. Then like magic, poof!" Bull threw up his hands in the dramatic gesture a magician makes when making a rabbit disappear. "The mafia families pull a switch."

"A switch? What kind of a switch?" Ward leaned back and stared at his partner.

Bull reached into his pocket and pulled out a copy of another article from the Seawood newspaper. The headline read "Town Council Reverses Its Decision." "Two months after the Council denies the Dwyers their appeal, it calls a special meeting and, get this, lawyers representing both the Gerberti and the Agrelo families show up and request that the Dwyer family be given back their dock space, the very space the Agrelo family had just won."

Ward shook his head as if his ears were stuffed with cotton. "Say again? Who shows up and does what?"

Bull scanned down a page of his notes. "Here it says, lawyers representing Old World Charter Cruises and Sea Wolf Enterprises announce they are withdrawing their applications for docking space."

"Did they give a reason?"

"Well if you believe in the tooth fairy, then you will definitely buy this. They said and I quote: "We wish to support the tradition of small family enterprises and we believe our own, larger cruise boats would detract from the overall ambiance of the area.""

"Ambiance? I thought you said the Seawood area was little more than rotting piers?"

"Yeah, I did. I'm told the place was a dump. I almost laughed out loud in the court library when I read that." Bull chuckled.

"So, the Dwyer fishing hole is back in business?"

Bull closed one eye and pointed his index finger at Ward, indicating he was right on target. "Better than that, the family is granted a 100-year-lease."

Gallery of the Chosen

Ward leaned back in his chair and narrowed his eyes. "Let me see if I've got this right. The Agrelo family wins the Dwyer docking space, and the Dwyers appeal but lose their appeal. Then lawyers for these competing families show up and insist that the Council reverse its decision and support the Dwyer appeal." Ward paused, trying to make sense out of the whole thing.

"Boss, this is screwy. You told me these were competing families."

Ward nodded. "They were and still are, as far as I know. Why would they cooperate and why would they help the Dwyers?"

"Exactly. So I figure at least there would be some nasty stuff after both families had time to consider what they had done, but nothing happens. All goes quiet, and both sides lose interest."

Ward laughed out loud. "Lose interest? What are they putting in that candy bar?"

"Nothing you need worry about. Anyway, nothing happens—no muscle, no bodies, nothing. The families take their cruise businesses farther out on the Island. And they live happily ever after. End of story."

"Nothing happened?"

"Nothing happened."

"Are you sure?" Ward challenged.

Bull looked hurt by Ward's question. "Boss, it's me!"

"Those families had been killing each other for decades." Ward stared into space. "This does not make sense, unless the Dwyers were somehow serving both families?"

"How would they do that?"

"I have no idea, but I know someone who might know. By the way, was there anything in the papers or court records about the Dwyers being involved in anything illegal?"

Bull shook his head. "Nothing. They're squeaky clean. Where do we go from here?" His voice raised an octave whenever he sensed something important was about to happen.

"Let's pay a visit to Jeff Keller. Maybe he can make sense out of this."

Bull eyed the remaining candy bar. "Is our meeting officially over?"

Ward smiled. "Yes, why?"

Bull reached out and removed the rest of the candy bar from its wrapper. "So, if I eat this now, I technically win the bet?"

Ward smiled and nodded. "You win the bet."

Smiling, Bull popped the candy into his mouth.

Chapter 11: Lieutenant Jeff Keller

During the entire drive into New York City Bull peppered Ward with a thousand questions about his early career as a police officer and detective. Bull wanted to fast track his own development into a first class detective. Ward smiled and reminded Bull that patience was a virtue the best detectives mastered. Bull paused briefly and then resumed peppering questions.

Ward's spirits lifted as he pulled his car into the precinct's parking lot. It felt good to be back with his friends.

Bull was given a brief tour of the police offices and then joined Ward, Keller and some of Ward's former colleagues in the coffee room where they were reminiscing about Ward's rookie years on the force. Lieutenant Keller was a burly six-footer from the Lower East Side who wore his thick New York accent like a badge of honor. He had the kind of face that could freeze you in your tracks, the kind of face you didn't mess with. He was famous for staring punks down, and getting them to break without so much as a word.

"There was this time," Keller said, looking directly at Bull, "when your partner here, just back from his honeymoon, forgot to load his gun and discovered it was empty only after he had nabbed a local thief at gun point."

"Seems I've conveniently forgotten that event," Ward added as he joined in the general laughter.

Jim Edgewood, who had worked closely with Ward during the early years, added: "One time your partner here walks up to this apartment complex over by the Hudson and was trying to find the buzzer to someone's apartment. Out comes this monster of a guy who thinks our boy here is with the Feds come to pay him a social call. So, next thing you know the two of them are rolling on the grass, punching it out. Ward told us later he had no idea who the guy was or why the guy jumped him. A squad car drives by and two more officers get into the mix. But the kicker was that the guy Ward had come to question shows up and when he sees the police cuffing Ward's wrestling partner, he takes off with our hero here in pursuit.

"It was a marathon. Ward chased his guy clear up to the Lincoln Center where he tackled him."

Keller smiled and feigned frustration. "Damned if Ward didn't get credit for apprehending two criminals and solving two cases in a single day."

Ward held up one hand to silence everyone. "Let's not forget that our good Lieutenant Keller did get mentioned in my report."

Keller chuckled. "Oh yeah. I seem to remember the words backup assistance somewhere in your report. "Backup assistance" my ass! Well, one thing is for damn sure," Keller said as he, Ward and Bull stood to leave for lunch at the precinct's favorite Bar and Grille, "Bull has better taste in clothes than you ever did." Bull's face beamed like a hot summer sun.

Paddy's Bar and Grille off of 14th Street is a dark, cavernous restaurant with old mahogany walls and worn-out leather-covered booths in the front, and no nonsense wooden tables and chairs in the back behind a half partition. The lights are dimmed and the windows shaded. If someone wanted to drink or have a private conversation, Paddy's would fit the bill. The boys at the precinct had their favorite tables in the back unofficially reserved twenty-four seven.

Bull filled Keller in on what he had found out about the Dwyer, Agrelo and Gerberti families.

"So, what do you think?" Ward asked. "Could the Dwyers have been working both families?"

Keller shook his head as he tossed a peanut high in the air, catching it in his mouth at the last moment. "You're kidding, right? Nobody works both families and lives to reach their next birthday. Not now, not then. I don't have to tell you that. You know the score. Honestly, I don't know what the hell was going on out at Seawood. It sounds pretty weird actually. The only time those families spent time together was to fight it out or attend each other's funerals."

Ward and Bull laughed. Bull had been watching Keller closely, admiring his dexterity in tossing and catching peanuts in his mouth without looking up. Bull reached for a pretzel, and tossed it in the air. It bounced off his forehead onto the table and then onto the floor. Keller and Ward pretended they didn't see what just happened.

Keller continued, "So, I can't see why they would've cooperated to help out a small-time fishing business. Even if the Dwyers were related to one of the families, no way the other family would have pulled out of a possible lucrative business opportunity. Unless, of course, they both owed the Dwyers some favor."

Bull's ears picked up. "What kind of favor?"

"Christ knows! But if it was a favor, it had to be pretty big to get those two families to agree on anything. You were either with one family or the other, but not both. I remember hearing about those turf wars as a kid. Hell! That was before our time. Shit! That was before everybody's time. There's always some bastard wanting someone else's turf. I'm afraid I can't be much help. Most of those guys who would know are either dead or rotting in jail. You're talking ancient history here, Ward." Keller tossed another peanut and successfully caught it; then without saying a word or looking at Bull, he slowly pushed the basket of peanuts in Bull's direction.

Bull shook his head, indicating he had lost his appetite for snacks and tricks.

"But, hey, let me get you another beer." Keller waved his hand to get the bartender's attention. "Hey, Jerry!"

"No, two beers, that's my limit," Ward reminded Keller.

"Yeah, sorry. I forgot. Jerry, never mind. You okay?"

"I'm getting there. By the way, I don't suppose anything has turned up on the Gerberti and my wife's murder?" Ward rubbed the rim of his beer glass. He averted Keller's eyes.

Keller stared at Ward, frustration showing on his face. "You don't still believe they're responsible for Barbara's death, do you?" Keller turned to Bull, "Hey, talk some sense into your partner before he gets himself killed. Tell him there's no proof the Gerberti family was ever involved in what happened to his wife." Keller turned back to Ward. "Here, let me spell it out for you for the zillionth time. We found no link between Barbara's murder and the Gerberti and their drug business. Guys on the inside, who should know, told us they were not involved."

Ward continued to stare at this glass.

"Sure the family was pissed that you slowed down their shipments, but they weren't so pissed that they murdered your wife."

"Well, tell me who the hell did it then? What good are we if a guy can kill your wife and walk away?" Ward's raised voice drew the attention of customers in the front room.

Keller ignored his outburst while Bull shifted uneasily in his chair.

"Jesus, Ward," Keller lowered his voice. "We've been down this road a hundred times. The guys at the precinct have busted their humps trying to find the bastard who did it, but we believe you're backing the wrong horse. Ward, please drop it!" Keller reached for another peanut, sat back and shifted topics. "Anyway, you asked about the Rockaway territory, right?"

Ward nodded.

"Yeah, well the Poles and Russians have moved in, last I heard. I don't get out there much. When I was younger, the wife and I would go to Lundy's for lobster on our anniversary, but unless the hoods crossed the bridge, I didn't care who got killed over there. I was too busy keeping Manhattan safe for democracy or some crap like that to bother with the other boroughs."

"Does the name J. Lynks, mean anything to you?" Ward asked.

Keller thought for a moment. "Lynks? No. Who is he?"

"I'm not really sure, but his body may be buried where it shouldn't be. I am trying to make sense of what was going on behind the scenes in Rockaway, Queens and Seawood back then."

"We're talking nineteen thirties and forties, right?" Keller rubbed his forehead. "Jesus, Ward. Why don't you ask me something easy like where Hoffa's buried?"

They all laughed.

Keller drained his beer glass. "Well there was this kid, fresh out of law school. He would help us out with those territories. If I remember right, he came from that area."

"Let me guess, he could be dead," Ward chimed in before Keller got the words out of his mouth.

Keller smiled and Ward returned the compliment. "No, I believe he's still breathing. Let's go back to the office and I'll look him up."

###

Gallery of the Chosen

Bull checked out the gun collection and hobnobbed with some of the detectives, while Keller went rummaging through a storage room. He finally emerged with a file box that looked like it hadn't been opened in a hundred years. He blew the dust off the lid and started fingering through the yellowed files.

"Here he is!" Keller pulled out a folder and flipped through some pages. "Bernie Rapin. That's him—just a green kid lawyer when we first met, but he helped when he could."

"Any idea how I can find him?"

"Yeah," Keller looked at a sheet of paper stapled to the front of the file. He wrote down contact information on a card and handed it across the desk to Ward.

"Professor Rapin?"

Keller nodded. "Rapin gave up the trial business and became a law professor at Brooklyn C. He specializes in organized crime in New York, the Island, actually in the whole shebang. Great expert witness, I'm told."

Bull overheard Keller's last remark as he pulled up a chair. "You can get a degree studying organized crime? You mean I could become a professor?"

"Seems you can." Keller picked up the telephone and dialed the number. "Nice guy, Rapin."

Professor Rapin was in his office and said he would wait, but had to leave by 6 p.m.

Ward stood up. "We better get going. We don't want to keep Professor Rapin waiting." They bid Keller goodbye and Ward promised they would return soon. He held the door open for his partner. "After you, Professor Toolman."

Bull's face lit up. "Professor Toolman. I like the sound of that! Of course I'll have to buy a whole new wardrobe." Bull straightened his back and puckered his lips suggesting he was either deep in thought or had just sucked on a lemon.

Peter Saunders

Chapter 12: Professor Rapin

Professor Bernie Rapin's office was off Flatbush Avenue in the basement of a run-down university building in Brooklyn. His room was a little bigger than a closet and barely had room for a desk, a swivel chair, one bookcase, a metal filing cabinet and a cheap metal chair with a seat the size of a placemat. A broken tablet arm dangling by a single screw hung from the metal chair. There were no windows and the distinct smell of raw sewage hung in the air. Professor Rapin, a heavyset man, made the room look even smaller. His faded green sweater barely stretched over his enormous belly and his corduroyed slacks were wrinkled beyond recognition. He had a full beard that he occasionally stroked, giving him a distinguished appearance from the neck up. Empty Styrofoam cups littered his desk and bookshelves. Examination papers, student essays, textbooks and journals were balanced precariously on every remaining surface and occasionally spilled over onto the floor, snaking their way along the baseboards. Bull and Ward stood in the hallway, peering in, wondering where they were going to sit.

Ward knocked on the open door. "Professor Rapin? I'm Ward Emerson. This is my partner, Vincent Toolman."

Bernie Rapin looked up from the student paper he was reading and set it aside. "Yes, yes. I was expecting you. You've saved me from reading another awful essay, a fate I wish on no one." Professor Rapin scanned his tiny room. "I didn't know there would be two of you." He offered to move some of the piles of books into the hallway and search for another chair, but Bull said he would rather stand. "But before we leave, if you have time, I want to ask you about how I can become a professor of crime."

"Well, I can tell you how I became a law professor specializing in studying the gritty underworld, if that will help." Rapin leaned back in his chair. It squeaked each time he moved. "It's lucky Jeff called when he did; I'm not usually in my dungeon of an office." He saw the surprised look on Bull's face as he surveyed the room.

"Sad, isn't it? Sorry, but I'm not into house cleaning. If the university is going to put faculty in dumps like this, they shouldn't expect us to spend much time here. It's a crime that the high tuition and fees they charge never seem to make a difference to faculty offices and classrooms. It's highway robbery if you ask me. They will tell you that all the money goes to faculty salaries so they can't improve the buildings, but I welcome anyone to look at what they pay me." Rapin sniffed the air. "Did you notice the stench when you came down the stairs?"

Ward nodded. Bull added, "Yeah, it stinks."

Rapin chuckled. "Toolman, I like you. I like a man who calls it as he smells it. The stench keeps most students and administrators away, so I have to consider the tradeoffs. But I'm boring you. How can I help?"

Ward told Rapin about the Dwyer case and the strange behavior of the Gerberti and Agrelo families out at Seawood.

Rapin thought for a minute, and then said, "Well, I was only a graduate student then. Most of those family members are doing time in the great hereafter." He smiled and continued. "The Gerberti and Agrelo families went at it pretty good in the early days and were still at it when I graduated from law school."

"Do you have any idea why competing families would suddenly decide to cooperate and support the Dwyers?" Ward asked.

Rapin stroked his beard several times giving full thought to Ward's question. "Not really. If anyone else had told me this story, I would've said they were delusional. Some pretty nasty stuff went on back then; cooperation was not a word I would use to describe their behavior. I know both families were active along the shores of Brooklyn and Long Island. The police suspected the boats were doing more than gambling. Rumor had it some of the boats smuggled in booze from Canada and drugs from Cuba. Gambling was just one of their pastimes."

"Any arrests?" Ward wondered aloud.

"Enough to satisfy the politicians and the newspapers," Rapin smirked. "A few raids but the police only went after small potatoes, punks selling booze without licenses, nothing solid enough to convict anyone on the bigger crimes. The Dwyer name doesn't ring a bell, but like I said, I had my head in the books, so there could be a link. I just don't know what it could be."

Gallery of the Chosen

"What can you tell me about the Gerberti family?"

"Plenty. They were part of my dissertation. What do you want to know?"

"I'm not sure yet, so anything you tell us could be helpful."

Rapin began rocking back and forth, his chair squeaking each time he leaned back. "The Gerberti was one of the earliest families to come over and settle in the area. The grandfather opened a tailor shop that was strictly legit. His first son, Ernesto, got in with some real winners and started a small extortion business. Later, another son, Salvatore, joined his brother. Ernesto was eventually found at Coney Island on the Cyclone ride with a bullet in his head. Salvatore and some friends then went on a killing spree. There was a younger brother, Rafael. The family called him the scholar. He preferred reading and teaching literature to killing, an interesting choice, right? Anyway, he didn't figure into the picture at all. The family left him to his Milton and Shakespeare. As the family business improved, they moved to Queens and from there onto the Island. I'm told the grandson, Antonio, now runs the business. Salvatore died of cancer five years ago. Rafael may still be alive, but he would be quite old."

Ward told Rapin about the stolen paintings from Barkley's estate and Barbara's death. He asked Rapin if he had heard anything that might connect the Gerberti to either of these cases.

"I'm sorry to hear about your wife. Frankly I'm surprised you think the Gerberti might have murdered her. Murder is not their thing these days and with all the heat they have been getting the last few years, murdering the wife of a former member of the force would have been a pretty stupid thing to do. I knew Antonio was making waves in Westchester, but that had more to do with drugs not works of art and certainly not murder. I doubt if any of the Gerberti, except Rafael maybe, have the brains to pull off an art heist and distribute the goods. They would need professional help."

"Like an international syndicate?" Ward suggested.

"Yeah, then it's a different story. But hey, this isn't a science. Organized crime is like a mutating organism. Just when you think you have identified all the parts and understand how it works and where its hiding places are, it changes shape. That's when it turns into something else, something you wouldn't expect—like a shipping or drug company. Scratch it and you'd be surprised at what you'll find. Organized crime is a regular shape-shifter."

Rapin blushed. "Sorry for the lecture. I sometimes forget I'm not in class. No one can be absolutely sure of anything when it comes to organized crime." He leaned back, forcing his chair back as far as it could go. The creaking sound suggested he was testing the laws of physics. The sound of straining metal hinted that he and the chair had reached a critical point.

Ward looked down at some notes he had brought with him "What about Jimmy D'Rosso? He's been linked indirectly to art heists. I've heard rumors that a local family he was working for had him doing the dirty work for an international syndicate."

Rapin paused for a moment to collect his thoughts. "Yeah, I know D'Rosso. He's doing time upstate. He was on the fringe of money laundering and fraud, or stolen artwork. But he was a foot soldier, a mere delivery boy. If he was involved, he was following someone else's orders. I wouldn't pin my hopes on D'Rosso as the brains behind anything. No, if anyone knows who's who in the world of art heist on both sides of the pond, your man would be Patrick O'Hare. He free-lances for families smart enough to see the long-term economic potential in paintings and the value of never asking where O'Hare acquired the work. He worked for the Gandante family on a couple of projects involving stolen art."

"What's he like?"

"O'Hare? Oh, he's a study, all right. He has a reputation as a real art connoisseur who spends most of his time at gallery openings and art shows, that's when he's not conning someone or painting. I hear he's a pretty good artist himself. I guess he'd have to be since he specializes in producing copies of lesser-known masterpieces held in private collections like the ones this Barkley fellow lost. He steals originals, copies them and sells his copies through the black market. It's all an under-the-table sort of thing. As I said, many of the buyers don't care if what they are buying is stolen, they think they're getting a bargain for a minor masterpiece and that's all they care about. O'Hare even has the balls to sell his copies back to the people he stole the originals from. His copies are so good, the buyers never suspect."

Bull couldn't contain himself. "You mean to say his customers are the people he has stolen the originals from?"

"A lot of them are. That's right. He even charges them a stiff finder's fee for negotiating with the thief—himself. O'Hare has the gift of gab; he's a creative genius at convincing unsuspecting buyers that they're getting the real thing. His other trick is pretending he represents rich widows short on cash who must sell their prized artwork. He tells his potential buyers all must be hush-hush because no one must know just how desperate these pillars of society are. The best part of his con is that his copies are so good that all hell doesn't break out unless someone tries to sell their masterpiece, or make a presentation to a museum. And sometimes even the experts can't tell the real thing from O'Hare's copies unless they spend top dollar analyzing the work under the microscope. The best part is those who do discover they have been taken for a ride don't want publicity, so they don't approach the police."

Ward smiled. "So he's talented?"

"Talented, crooked, persuasive and quite charming: a winning combo. A half a million bucks say he knows which syndicate is working in Westchester and who's got Barkley's paintings. Who knows, he might have had Barkley's collection lifted himself."

"Know where I can find him?"

"Sure, Pat is doing time in Jersey. He turned himself in, a few years ago."

"Was O'Hare ever linked to the Gerberti or Gandante families?"

"No, he likes to work on his own and is too smart to spill what he knows. He knew the system wouldn't let him rot in prison. A federal district judge dealt the prosecutors a major blow by barring O'Hare's testimony."

"On what grounds?"

"I don't remember, but I know the decision weakened the government's case and bang, nothing big stuck. So, Pat is doing a light sentence in Jersey. But don't bet on him telling secrets. From what I hear, he's in love."

"In love? I don't understand."

Rapin smiled. "That's right. Some woman he met in England while he was casing a private collection has smitten his heart with her beauty. He's up for parole in a couple of years, so anything he says could cost him leg and limb when he gets out. Therefore mum's the word with O'Hare. She's all he thinks about from what I hear."

"Anything else you can tell me that might help?" Ward stood to go.

"Yeah, don't believe anything he says if he does talk. He is very, very convincing, but he is a major liar. Could've been a politician."

They all laughed.

"What about the Dwyer case? Is there anyone who might be able to help me with what went on between the families in that area years ago?"

"Well, the big players are either dead or too smart to tell, but there were a number of petty crooks who did odd jobs for the families out there; they moved around and did what was needed. One of them might know."

"Would you know where I might find any of these guys?"

Rapin carefully maneuvered his chair around, turned to his filing cabinet, and searched through some files. "Let's see, yeah, here's the list."

Rapin scanned his list of names. "Man, this goes way back. I don't know how many of these guys are still kicking." Then he paused and stared at one name. "Good God, Luis Bertini. I forgot all about poor Luis. According to my last entry he lived in Brooklyn and was involved with the numbers racket in the Bay Ridges area." Rapin flipped to another page. "Bingo, says here he worked for the Gerberti family in Sheepshead Bay and in Seawood before he went into the Army. He did some petty numbers running and small time crime, but nothing big. He was only a kid, sixteen, seventeen tops. But he would have been working for them around the time the Dwyer family was losing their dock space."

Rapin scanned more of his notes. "Yeah, I definitely remember Luis. Came across him when I was in Brooklyn, but I don't think he will be much help."

"Is he dead?" Bull asked.

Rapin shook his head. "Well, that depends on what you mean by dead. Luis suffered brain damage during the war. A shell landed as his platoon was decamping. Killed just about everyone but Luis. Opened a huge hole in his skull. How he survived no one knows. They had to sew part of his brain back together. He was in a coma for nearly a month and couldn't remember anything new when he came out of the coma. Unfortunately he didn't get any better after the operations."

"Amnesia?"

"No, that's what's so strange about his condition. He couldn't retain anything new, but he remembered everything that happened to him before the shell went off. Poor bastard is frozen in the past. His mother hired me to get him medical benefits. That's how I came across him. His was one of my first cases. He must be in his late seventies by now. Kind of creepy."

"How so?"

"Well, if I remember right, Luis still thought he was in the Army when I met him five years after he had been discharged. Like I said, he was stuck in the past. Without memory, there isn't a hell of a lot to hang your sense of self on, if you know what I mean. Luis's memories were the only self he had left."

"But he could remember the past?"

"Yeah, crystal clear, but that's all he could remember. Nice kid. Sad, really sad."

"Know where I might find him?"

"Yeah, he was at a nursing home out on the Island. His mother would have passed away years ago." Rapin wrote the name and address of the nursing home on a slip of paper.

"Does the name J. Lynks ring a bell?"

Rapin drew a blank and nothing turned up in his files.

"Professor Rapin you have been very helpful."

Rapin struggled out of his chair, reached over and shook Ward's hand, and as he shook Bull's hand he asked, "You wanted to ask me some questions about becoming a professor? Are you sure you want to become one? You may end up in a dump like this."

Bull shook his hand. "Never mind."

Rapin sat down and smiled up at Bull. "The smell down here kind of kills your appetite for higher learning, doesn't it? If I can help again don't hesitate to call."

Rapin waved as Ward and Bull left his office. He picked up the essay he had been reading, leaned back and continued testing the limits of his chair.

Chapter 13: Luis Bertini

Two days later, Ward drove to the Island. He had located the nursing home and discovered Luis Bertini was still there. He planned to swing by the home, pay his respects to Bertini, pump him with a few questions, and then head back to New Rochelle. It would be just a quick routine visit.

From the road below, the nursing home was hidden from view by thickets of wild shrubs and trees. Up ahead to the left of the highway, a faded sign directed Ward up a narrow road squeezed between rows of twisted trees to a twenty-story brick building perched high on a hill facing the ocean. The building looked more like a condemned tenement than a nursing home. Its exterior was covered with peeling flakes of institutional grey paint. A front garden that once might have been manicured had been abandoned and become a tangled sea of brush surrounding a badly weathered war memorial where three stone soldiers leaned forward, their arms extended toward the ocean, pointing to some phantom ship returning from war. The weathered figure of a nurse stood behind them, her gaze fixed on her patient seated in a wheelchair. What were once shiny sculptures were now ghostly, forgotten specters, horribly streaked by rivulets of weather and time. A dark and cloudy sky contributed to the ghostly appearance of everything.

Ward parked, entered the building and approached the front desk. "I'm here to see Mr. Luis Bertini. Can you tell me where I might find him?"

The volunteer looked surprised at Ward's request and glanced at a large wall clock. "You'll find him in the visitor's lounge, tenth floor. At this time, he's always in the visitor's lounge. Take the elevator down the hall to the right."

Ward took the elevator as directed. As he stepped off and into the hall, he spotted an attendant reading a newspaper. He was an African American in a crisp, white uniform, and was seated outside a lounge. As Ward approached, the attendant jumped up as if he had been caught loafing on the job. He towered over Ward.

"I'm here to see Luis Bertini. Can you tell me where he is?"

The attendant pointed into the darkened lounge. "He's in there. Mr. Luis doing fine, real fine."

"That's good," Ward said, not knowing what else to say.

"You family?" the attendant asked.

"No, just an acquaintance."

"Lord, I'm glad to see someone's come. Mr. Luis, he don't get many visitors since his mama passed away."

"How long ago was that?"

"Oh, seven or eight years ago, I guess. Only one come now is Mr. R. He been coming since Mr. Luis's mama died."

"Mr. R? Who's that?"

The attendant seemed to hesitate at Ward's question.

"If you tell me his name, maybe I know him?" Ward added.

"Mr. R. is the name he go by. Don't know his real name. He a nice man, real gentleman. He pay me real good."

Ward stared at the attendant. "He pays you? You're not paid by the nursing home?"

The attendant's face broke into a wide grin. "Hell no, can't live on what they pays you. No sir. Mr. R, he pays me real good to take care of Mr. Luis full time."

"What does Mr. R. look like?"

"He's old, like Mr. Luis, only he has bad legs, uses a cane. Has fish eyes."

Ward raised an eyebrow. "Has what?"

"Fish eyes; he nearly blind, I guess. Wears thick glasses. Makes his eyes bubble out big, like fish eyes. Mister, if you want to visit Mr. Luis you better go in 'cause visiting hours, they almost done."

Ward peered into the lounge and looked back at the attendant. "Why aren't the lights on?"

"Mr. Luis, he likes it that way. Calms him."

Ward thanked the attendant and went into the poorly lit, cavernous lounge, which was empty except for the solitary figure of Bertini sitting in a large green, vinyl chair. He was staring out the window. Luis smiled and stood up as Ward approached. Reaching out, he took Ward's hand and shook it vigorously. Although he was in his late seventies with grey hair and a face full of wrinkles, he was full of animation when he spoke. Bertini had the eyes of a much younger man. "Are you a doctor?" he asked.

"No, I'm not a doctor. I'm Ward Emerson."

"I didn't think so; you're not wearing a white coat. Is it time for me to go?"

"Go? Go where?"

"Back to the front. Is it time for me to go back to the front?"

Ward looked away, his heart sinking at the horrible joke nature had played on this old man. "Luis, do you know what year this is?"

"Of course I know what year it is. Hell, we're in the middle of a war. Forty-four, that's what year it is. This is a hospital, isn't it?"

"It's a nursing home."

Luis began rubbing his forehead. "I remember my buddies and I were shelled. That's why I'm here, isn't it?"

"Yes."

"But I don't feel sick. Am I sick?"

"I don't know, Luis. You'll have to ask your doctor."

Luis looked around the room. "I don't see anyone from my platoon, so I guess they got out okay. I was always unlucky that way, you know. If anyone fell down in the schoolyard and scrapped his knee, it was Luis." He ran his fingers through his silver hair and smiled. "Funny isn't it, how some guys are always unlucky that way? But I think I'm getting better and should be going back to my unit soon. That's what I told my mother, but she hasn't been here today. Is she coming today?"

Ward suddenly felt trapped, his stomach tightened. "I don't know."

"Hey, can you tell me why I'm in here with all these old people? I think I must work here. Do I work here?"

"Maybe."

Luis went to the window and put his hand on the glass as if he were touching the sea beyond. "I'm going back to Belmont after the war and make some real money. I was doing pretty well before I got drafted. As soon as the war is over, I'm going back to the track."

"The Belmont race track?"

"Yeah, you've been there?"

"No, I've never been to Belmont."

Louis turned and faced Ward, his eyes and face lit up with anticipation. "I can't wait. You should go sometime. It's a great place."

Ward wanted to ask his questions and get out of there. "Luis, I heard you worked on the fishing boats out at Seawood. Do you like to fish?"

"What?"

"Do you like to fish?"

"Fish? I think I do. A couple of my friends, we fish for blues at Seawood. Nice place Seawood. I worked on some of the boats out there a couple of years before I got the job at the track."

"Did you work for the Dwyer family?"

Luis's smile vanished when he heard the Dwyer name. He turned back to the window and looked out. "No, I didn't work for them. Who told you that?" Luis's hand began patting the glass window.

"But you knew the Dwyer family, didn't you, Luis?"

"Yeah, I knew them, but I never worked for them. Don't know anything about that." Suddenly Luis returned to his chair and seemed lost in his thoughts. Then he looked up at Ward and gave him a sheepish smile. "I got some friends at the track who will help me make good money. I'm going to get married. I've got a girlfriend, a real looker."

Ward's heart sank. Coming here was a colossal mistake. He started to leave, but hesitated and decided to ask Luis one final question.

"Luis, is Lynks one of your friends?"

Luis's complexion turned ashen as a look of recognition and fear crossed his face. "Who?"

"J. Lynks? Did you know him?"

Luis began rocking back and forth. He gripped the arms of the chair, digging his fingernails deep into the vinyl. He avoided Ward's gaze. "Yeah, I knew Johnny. But I couldn't do anything. I heard the cries, but I didn't know what was going on. So I ran. I swear I didn't do anything." Luis was pleading now and started to cry. He covered his face with his hands. His body rocked faster. "Please don't, please don't hurt me. I didn't know. I swear, I didn't know. I won't tell, I promise." He held his arms up to protect himself, as if expecting Ward to strike him.

"I'm not going to hurt you. Luis, listen to me." Ward approached to comfort and reassure him, but Luis suddenly jumped up and while trying to escape fell forward, hitting his head hard against the window as his body slid to the floor. A smear of blood down the window traced his decent.

Ward raced over, lifted Luis off of the floor helping him back to the chair. Blood streaked his forehead as a few drops fell on his hand. When Luis saw the blood he screamed and panicked. He jumped up, pushed Ward aside and ran toward the door and right into the arms of the attendant who came running when he heard Bertini's cry. By the time Ward had recovered, the attendant had grabbed Luis's head between his hands and shoved his own face right up against Luis's. He shouted at him, "Hey, Luis. You're in the Army now, right? Are you in the Army, Luis?"

Luis's wild, terrified eyes stared at the attendant for a moment. He then calmed down and seemed to have no recollection of what had just happened. The attendant helped him back to his chair and held a handkerchief to his brow.

Ward took a deep breath. He was covered with sweat and his hands shook. He felt dizzy and sick to his stomach.

Returning to his genial self, Luis smiled up at Ward. The attendant checked the bleeding; it had stopped.

"I'm going back to the track when the war is over. Hey, what happened to my head?" He looked hard at Ward. "Are you a doctor?"

"No, I'm not a doctor."

The attendant nodded that Ward should leave. Their eyes met and the attendant whispered, "You won't tell Mr. R. about this, will you?"

"No, I won't tell him. Luis, I have to leave now."

Ward started for the door, but Luis intercepted him and grabbed one of Ward's hands. He shook it vigorously. "Hey, it was nice meeting you. When the war is over, I'm going to get married."

"Okay, Luis." Ward turned and left. Whose cries did Luis hear? Lynks'? Maybe Lynks had stumbled on illegal operations the Dwyer family was involved in. The way Luis reacted suggested he may have witnessed Lynks' murder and had been hiding at the racetrack until he got drafted.

Ward was certain there was more Luis could tell him, but he couldn't face him again. Something about Luis had gotten to him.

Outside, Ward went behind the building and threw up. A feeling of dread had taken hold of him and wouldn't let go. He needed to get home, to get away from this place. Ward started his car and headed back to New Rochelle. *I needed to ask him those questions,* Ward told himself. *That's why I came here.* But something deep inside Ward would not buy it. *I never should have asked him about Lynks. I should have left him alone, left him in his peaceful world, dreaming about the good days he would have with a girl, a racetrack and a future that had already passed him by.*

Chapter 14: Letting Go

Winter had come on hard, delivering a series of ice storms from Jersey to Maine, crippling trains and buses, humbling even the most hardened of souls. Main Street New Rochelle was practically deserted except for two men digging a car out of a snow bank. Ward's car crept along at ten miles an hour. The driveway that led to Dr. Morgan's office had not been plowed and snow piled high at the curbs made parking impossible. Her car was nowhere to be seen, but a light in her office window told him she would be there.

He pulled his car as close to the curb as possible and climbed out, his legs disappearing into snow up to his knees. He trudged his way up the hill and went directly to her office.

While Cynthia acknowledged and observed the rituals of her profession, everywhere he looked he could see signs of her positive spirit peeking out, touching everything. She had decorated her office for the holidays. Ornaments hung from the potted fir tree in the corner while a string of Christmas lights snaked its way around and through its branches, casting soft and pleasing shades of light against the wall. A menorah candelabrum was displayed on a side table. Cynthia was playing her favorite holiday recording of a choir singing. Ward pulled off his boots and removed his coat. Cynthia opened her office door.

"You made it."

"Merry Christmas."

"Happy holidays. Come in." Cynthia went to her chair and picked up her notepad while Ward took his seat. She reached across her desk, turned the music off, and then opened her notebook to a new page. "Your message sounded urgent when you called. What's going on?"

Ward recounted his visit to see Bertini and the impact it had on him.

"I've read about cases of Korsakov's syndrome," Cynthia responded.

"What is it?" Ward asked, a note of nervousness creeping into his voice.

"Well, the patient cannot remember isolated incidents for more than a few seconds. It usually results from severe head injuries. His dates back to the explosion. You say you are frightened by Bertini's condition. Do you think you might end up like him?"

Ward scoffed at the idea. "Of course not, that's why I can't explain why I get anxious thinking about the way he is."

"What frightens you about him? Can you pinpoint what it is?"

"I keep thinking about the horrible trap he's in."

"Trap? Do you mean his mental condition or his confinement or both?"

"When he told me he was going to get married as soon as he was discharged, I felt this shock go through my body. I felt dizzy and sick."

"What was it that made you feel sick?"

Ward felt annoyed. "Come on, Cynthia. I don't know. Here is this guy, stuck in the past, and he doesn't know it. I mean the poor bastard really thinks he is going to marry someone who in all probability is dead. I feel for him. You know, I really feel for him. I guess I'm…" Ward's voice trailed off into silence.

Cynthia stopped writing. "You're what?"

"Nothing." Ward covered his face with his hands.

"No, you were about to say something. What? What were you about to say?"

Ward's voice shook. "I'm like Bertini. That's what I was about to say. I want to keep living with Barbara, but she's gone. I'm alone and lost without her, but I've been waiting. Waiting for what? She was taken from me and I feel trapped. But there's nothing to wait for, is there? I'm like Bertini. I'm waiting for something that will never happen, and someone who is no longer alive. Barbara's gone."

"Yes, she's gone and you can't bring her back. But you're not like Bertini. You still have years of life left. Unlike Bertini, you can go on living in the present, whereas he is trapped in the past. You're not trapped. But you have to let go."

Ward felt exhausted.

Cynthia accepted the silence between them and waited for Ward to move forward.

"I know you are right, but…"

"But what?" Cynthia continued.

"I can't let go until I catch Barbara's murderer."

"And why is that?"

"Because I feel responsible for her death. I owe her that."

Cynthia looked directly at Ward but remained silent. He didn't have to ask; he knew what she was thinking. "I know what you're going to say."

"Okay, what was I going to say?"

"You were about to say that I know better."

"And do you?" she asked with a slight smile appearing.

"Yeah. I know I'm not responsible. I know that. But I'll feel better when I catch her killer."

"Ah, that's different, Ward. Yes, you'll feel better when you catch Barbara's murderer. It's good you can see the difference. Tell me about Michelle, the woman you recently met. You told me that you thought she liked you and that you had some interest in her. Is that still true?"

Ward took a deep breath. "I do like her and she seems interested in me, but..."

"But? There's that word again. Do you talk to her?"

"Of course I talk to her."

"You know what I mean. Have you let Michelle know that you're interested in her not just as a friend but romantically?"

"No."

"Well, when were you going to tell her?"

"After."

"After what?"

"After I've caught Barbara's murderer."

Cynthia paused. The expression on her face indicated she was studying him, measuring what she would say next. "Ward, what if you don't catch him?"

Cynthia's words stung him deeply. Bertini's face flashed before him. If he didn't catch her murderer, he could end up like Bertini, forever searching, forever waiting for his life to begin again. The years would tick by and then . . .

Ward looked at Cynthia. "Not finding Barbara's murderer is not an option; it's not something I can accept."

"I understand, but if you don't let Michelle know how you feel, she may get the wrong impression. She may think you don't feel anything for her. Do you agree?"

Cynthia was pointing to a door Ward knew he had to walk through.

"I'm afraid that if I get too close to her, someone might hurt her."

"Like they hurt Barbara?"

"Yes."

"So, you cannot really ever be involved with another woman again if you believe that, can you?"

Ward didn't answer.

"Do you see the position you've put yourself in by blaming yourself for Barbara's murder?"

Ward nodded.

"So, when do you see Michelle again?" Cynthia asked.

"There's a farewell party for Willard Rhodes, a local sailing celebrity. It's this weekend."

"And Michelle will be there?"

"Yes."

"Well, this sounds like a perfect opportunity to break the ice with her, don't you think?" Cynthia glanced at the clock. "Our time is up, but Ward, I hope you go to that party. Tell Michelle how you feel."

All energy had drained from Ward's body. He carefully made his way home, stretched out on the couch and fell into a deep sleep. He dreamed of a trip his family had taken to a cabin by a lake in New Hampshire. He was fourteen or fifteen years old, and one evening when the family was asleep, he remembered making his way out of the cabin and down to the dock. He sat watching the mist rise on the lake and the million stars above. Suddenly a loon called out. A few moments later another loon—probably its mate—called back. He remembered feeling there was a note of sadness in the calls. Again the first loon called out and again the mate's response came back, but faded as the bird flew high into the night and disappeared over the mountain. Another call echoed across the lake, but there were no more responses.

Chapter 15: Michelle

Willard Rhodes, affectionately known as Will, was a former commodore of a prestigious Westchester yacht club. He had won more boat races than anyone else on either side of Long Island Sound. Recently, he had retired from his Manhattan law firm and was taking part in an international regatta in the Caribbean. He would be gone all winter. There was to be a small farewell party at Two Toms Tavern, organized by fellow sailors and acquaintances like Ward who had done some work for Willard's firm over the years.

Ward fidgeted with his tie pulling it this way and that way, trying to get the knot to sit straight. He couldn't believe how nervous he was. He felt like a schoolboy on his first date, except he didn't really have a date. He couldn't kid himself; the nervousness was because Michelle would be there. Some connection between them had begun to take root and although he tried to resist the attraction, he had failed miserably. Perhaps it was the soft smile that appeared whenever they met, but at some mysterious moment, Ward's heart began to awaken from its terrible sleep.

He pulled the tie off and started over.

Dr. Morgan's comment about needing to let Michelle know his feelings made sense. Was he this nervous when he dated Barbara? What the hell would he say to Michelle? Why wouldn't this stupid knot stay straight?

###

Sounds of singing drifted out into the evening air, greeting Ward as he carefully made his way up the shoveled side path to the tavern's back entrance. Michelle's dog Mo, a great lab, greeted Ward with a halfhearted, muffled bark and wagged his tail as Ward entered the tavern.

Batches of balloons and colored streamers dangling from the ceiling had given the usually dark lounge a festive atmosphere. A red spinnaker covering one entire wall was decorated with photos of Rhodes' racing yacht crossing the finish line in numerous important races. A few of his trophies were displayed on a table, as were photos of Will and his crews. A sign on the wall read "Set Sail, Old Salt! Do Your Mates Proud."

Ward found Michelle at the piano surrounded by Will and a group of his friends. She wore a pink silk blouse and black leather pants with a matching jacket. Silver earrings added to the overall knockout impression. Michelle had planned on being a ballerina. She was slim, with a long neck, a medium length torso, long legs and arms. There was something ethereal about her in the grace and fluidity of her movements that captured one's attention. But her college dance instructor told her she was too tall and would overshadow typical male partners. Elite school after elite school turned her down but praised her dancing. After a few years of knocking on doors, she turned to singing and playing the piano, but her beauty was undeniable.

Ward joined the others. She smiled at him, hitting the keys with authority as the song ended.

Except for Michelle, the others were terrible singers, and they knew it. "Although I'll miss you all," Will said, "I challenge anyone to find a kinder, more off-key group of singers this side of the Atlantic. Just don't give up your day jobs, boys and girls!"

"Don't fall overboard," someone called out.

"Hey, I don't drink and sail; I sail and drink," Will responded, turning to Tommy. "This round's on me."

Tommy smiled and headed for the bar.

Although Will was several years older than Michelle, everyone knew he had a crush on her and had invited her to join him on his trip. She said she would think about it, but apparently still hadn't made up her mind. Side bets had been placed on whether she would accept his offer. At the latest count, the odds were two to one that Michelle would be sitting at Will's side on the morning flight.

Gallery of the Chosen

"Dance time," Tom called out as he lowered the lights and signaled to Tommy to pipe in music from the bar. The crowd pushed the piano back and made a circle as a few patrons grabbed partners and began dancing. Taking Michelle's hand, Will led her onto the dance floor. Ward took a beer from a tray and sat down. He watched Will and Michelle move to the music, gliding gracefully around. Michelle's lithe body slowly swayed to the rhythms. Will whispered something in her ear and she smiled. Ward took a long, hard drink.

Tom went over to Tommy, said something to him, and then retreated back to the bar.

"She is something, isn't she?" Tommy said as he pulled up a chair next to Ward.

"What?" Ward answered.

Tommy leaned in and shouted in his ear. "Don't give me any of that what are you talking about crap. I don't have to be a detective to see what's what. You know who I'm talking about." He nodded in Michelle's direction. "As if you didn't notice that Michelle is beautiful. Did you know Will has asked her to join him on his trip to the Caribbean? Fifty bucks says she'll refuse." Tommy pulled out his wallet, removed five tens and slapped them on the table. Ward stared at the money.

"She would be nuts to turn him down. He's divorced, well-healed and from what I hear very, very generous." Ward took another stiff drink.

Tommy picked up his money and waved it under Ward's nose. "Still, I bet she stays."

Ward smiled and pushed the money away. "What the hell makes you so sure?"

Tommy pushed the money back under Ward's nose. "Let's just say I have bartender's instincts. Do we have a bet?"

"No." Ward dragged his chair far enough away so Tommy couldn't reach him. Tommy returned the money to his wallet and gave Ward a mysterious wink.

"Bartender's instinct? What a crock!" Ward said as they both laughed.

"Come on, big time gambler. Put up or shut up. Do we have a bet?" Tommy reached for his wallet again.

Ward knew that the only way to get his friend off his back was to accept the wager. Besides, he didn't mind losing the money if it meant Michelle would stick around. "Okay, you're on." Ward raised his glass to seal the bet.

The music had stopped and another dance number was beginning. Michelle had excused herself and gone to freshen up.

Will came over and joined Ward and Tommy. "Man, she's something."

Ward glanced at Tommy, who waved the wallet still in his hand. "So, has she accepted your offer?" Tommy asked as Will mopped perspiration from his face with a napkin.

Will looked briefly at his glass. "Not yet, but she told me she would let me know before the night's over." It was Will's turn to take a long drink as the music and the dancers started up again.

"Well, she's a fine catch for any man." Tommy added, "And if you ask me, a fellow would be out of his mind not to try to win her." Ward could feel Tommy's eyes staring right at him.

"I'll drink to that." Will raised his glass and Ward reluctantly did the same.

Tom came over and briefly joined the table. He winked at Tommy. "Did Will describe his strategy for the race?"

"Not yet." Tommy turned to Will. "I'd like to hear your plans for the big race."

Will began describing the course for his upcoming competition and was placing napkins and coasters strategically around the table indicating the various markers and tacks he hoped to take. Ward listened politely but kept wondering when Michelle would return. Finally, he spotted her weaving gracefully between dancers, heading in their direction. Tommy spotted her too and slid his chair in front of Will so he couldn't see Michelle's return. Tommy began peppering Will with questions about the race.

Michelle gave Ward a smile and took his hand in hers. "Can this lady have the next dance?"

The next thing Ward knew, he was holding Michelle in his arms. Her hair brushed his cheek and the touch of her hand caused his heart to pound. This is crazy, he told himself. He was a grown man, not some punk kid. But his heart kept pounding and there was nothing he could do about it.

Gallery of the Chosen

After a few tentative moments he pulled Michelle closer. Silently and meaningfully they moved together, back and forth, like the great tidal currents across the waters of the Sound. Their souls slowly, mysteriously bonded. Gently, Michelle's body responded to Ward's pull. It took his breath away.

"How long will you be gone?"

Michelle leaned back and studied Ward's expression. Then she put her cheek against his again. "Who said I was going anywhere? Are you trying to get rid of me?" She smiled briefly as they turned, aware that Will was studying her intensely.

"No, but I understand Will invited you to join him on his sail and. . . ." Ward couldn't think of what to say next. His heart was still pounding in his ears.

"Do you think I should go?" Michelle teased.

"Well, we would miss you."

"We? What about you? Would you miss me?"

Ward had to come clean. "Actually, I dread the thought of losing you. It's just that I have been struggling."

"I know." She looked into his eyes and gave him a hug. He held her close and closed his eyes.

"Since Barbara died. . . ."

"Shhh." Michelle put her finger to his lips. "It's okay. Don't say any more. When my husband left me, I nearly died. There were days I wished I had, but I didn't. It takes time, Ward, lots and lots of time. A broken heart doesn't heal quickly. What you're feeling is a very special kind of pain. You loved your wife and she was taken from you. My husband broke my heart. There's a difference."

Ward glanced over at Will who was sitting alone. From the way he was tapping his foot and staring in their direction, it was clear he wasn't happy. The song had ended and another had begun with Ward and Michelle still dancing together. Ward remembered what Cynthia had said about sharing his feelings with Michelle, and he considered Tommy's advice about winning Michelle's heart.

"So, if I want to invite this lady to dinner this week, will she still be here to accept my invitation?" Ward's heart froze for a second as he waited for her reply.

Michelle smiled. "Well, Mister Big Shot Detective, that depends."

Ward gave her a quizzical look. "Depends on what?"

"Depends on where you're taking me."

The dance continued and neither Ward nor Michelle noticed Will joining the other sailors at the bar. Ward didn't need to look for Tommy. He knew from the way Michelle held him that he owed Tommy fifty bucks.

Chapter 16: The Album

Dr. Morgan had encouraged Ward to begin putting the past behind him. All of Barbara's belonging had finally been given away and today he would put in storage the photos they collected over the years. From the top shelf of the closet he removed a large box that he placed on the dining room table and began sifting through its contents. There was a photo taken the day he met Barbara in Manhattan. Ward smiled, remembering how life in the city had seemed different from his sheltered life in Westchester and how Barbara taught him to really see the city as an insider.

All of his father's acquaintances were wealthy businessmen or politicians. Their sons and daughters were headed for Ivy League colleges, and all seemed to have been promised a place on the fast track to success. He was no different. Princeton, his father's alma mater, had accepted him and he did well, but his heart wasn't in it. Upon graduation, he decided he needed time to find himself, so instead of entering law school, he moved to the East Village. His father was furious, his mother sympathetic. "Take your time," she said. "You're ruining your life," his father countered.

After a year of working part-time jobs, Ward applied to the Police Academy and was accepted. At the Academy he quickly discovered he was seen as an outsider, a wealthy kid who didn't belong. He received a cool reception from many of the junior officers who came from poorer backgrounds. Why would someone from a rich family want to become a cop? They wanted what he was giving up. It just didn't make sense. Rumors spread that he would be pushed to the front of the line and promoted because of his father's connections. Ward didn't want his father's connections, but no one believed him. For a long time he was merely tolerated.

Lieutenant Jeff Keller was different. He didn't give a damn about Ward's privileged background. What Keller saw in Ward Emerson was dedication and a sharp mind. As long as Ward pulled his weight, Keller treated him like everyone else.

Keller had grown up on the Lower East Side and had been with the force ten years before Ward arrived. When Keller found out guys were betting that the rich kid wouldn't last a year, he picked Ward as his partner and things began to change for the better.

"Relax," Keller told Ward as they took a break at the local Dunkin Donut shop. "You don't have to be so serious, so focused all the time. Life's too short, have some fun."

Ward knew Keller was right; he needed to relax if he was going to fit in.

One Friday afternoon while Keller and Ward were poring over some case files, Keller presented Ward with an invitation. "A cousin of mine, a budding artist, is having a showing in the Village Saturday night. Why don't you come along? You'll meet some interesting people."

Ward didn't have his mother's passion for art, but he had learned to appreciate some valuable pieces she owned. He took Keller's advice and went to the party. He remembered feeling somewhat lost until a pretty, dark haired young woman walked up to him and handed him a glass of wine.

"Here, this will numb the pain. I'm Barbara Mendez."

"Is it that obvious?" I'm Ward Emerson."

"Well, Ward Emerson, let's just say you look like you're about to undergo a root canal." They both laughed. She was a graduate student studying art history at Hunter College.

The picture Ward held in his hand was a group photo of those who stayed till the end of the party. Barbara and Ward stood close together. We were so young, he thought, smiling at their outdated clothes. The photo reminded him of why he had fallen in love with Barbara. He loved her black hair, pretty face, her flair for choosing clothes that accented her figure and those long, lovely legs. But most of all, he loved her strong independent spirit, her openness to new things and new people, her gentleness, and her passion for her New York City.

Barbara had grown up in the Hispanic part of Brooklyn, although her family moved to Manhattan when she was ten. She was more cosmopolitan than Ward and over time taught him to see past the hype and glitz of Broadway which marketers promoted and outsiders swallowed as the essence of the city. Like all cities, New York reflected life at its best and worst.

Gallery of the Chosen

"Times Square is not what makes my city unique," Barbara said one day as they grabbed a hotdog from a street vendor near Pace College. "You have to dig and work to find the real New York. You have to earn it to become a member of the family. It's more a state of mind than a physical place. The real New York is everywhere, in all the boroughs, and in everything, just waiting to be mined."

Ward wasn't sure he understood what she meant until one Sunday afternoon while they were wandering through the Museum of Modern Art. Barbara pointed to a magnificent mosaic that covered an entire wall. Alternating ceiling spotlights created the impression of multiple forms constantly emerging from the mosaic's colored tiles, then blending back in with the overall pattern.

Ward had walked right past the piece, but circled back when he realized Barbara remained behind. "This is my New York," she said as she took him by the arm and led him forward till they stood side by side, their noses almost touching the mosaic. "Up close you appreciate the uniqueness of each piece of tile, of each ethnic group, each gender, each class, each point of view and each dream." Then she moved Ward back till they stood half way across the room. "Step back and take in the whole thing and there it is! This is my city." After that day, something wonderful had begun to happen to Ward, something that he couldn't explain. All he knew was that when he was in the city, he felt free.

Ward lifted another photo from the box, this time it was of his parents with Barbara, taken at his family's summer home upstate. His father's rigid, forced smile reminded Ward just how much his father disapproved of Barbara and her ethnic background. Ward could still feel how tense their meetings had been, how awkward the conversations and silences at the dinner table, and the uncomfortable greetings and goodbyes. "This girl is nothing but a gold digger," his father warned. Ward's mother, on the other hand, liked Barbara and enjoyed her company. Like everything and everyone, Barbara took them all in stride.

Somehow Barbara could calm the turbulent emotions from Ward's childhood that rolled in like high tide during a storm. If it hadn't been for her love and strength, where would his life have drifted he wondered?

It took him years before he found it in his heart to forgive his father for his drinking, his uncontrollable rages and physical abuse. One late summer evening, long after his father had retired from his company and divorced Ward's mother, Ward sat with his elderly father on the wide verandah of his Yacht club, drinks in hand, staring at the racing boats and yachts anchored off shore. A thin ribbon of moonlight stretched far out across the Sound.

Ward remembered thinking how terribly lonely and broken his father seemed. It was then that his father, a very private man, told him how he had suffered at the hand of his own drunken father. How, as a boy, he would climb out his bedroom window and hide in the woods behind the house to avoid his father's wrath. When he heard his mother crying he would cover his ears. Next morning he would sneak back to his bedroom. At breakfast, if his mother came out of her room, nothing would be said about her bruises and swollen lips, as if the violence had never happened. Like father like son, Ward's father also became a violent man. Ward was determined to break the horrible cycle of violence, and he succeeded.

It was Barbara who taught Ward to forgive his father. A year before his father died, Ward made his peace. It was the only time he saw his father cry. Ward learned to forgive, but he could never forget the violence and the damage it caused.

He lifted other photos from the box. He and Barbara had eloped, so there were no photos of their marriage before the justice of the peace. Later there were photos of them opening presents, greeting relatives and vacationing. Then, there was the last photo taken at dawn on their anniversary just as they were about to ascend in a hot air balloon above the Arizona desert. Ward stared at the final photo and leaned it against the desk calendar. He had to move on, but these memories he would keep forever.

His body jumped at the sudden ringing of the telephone.

"Ward, it's Bob Tilson. Sorry to call so early." Bob, also a detective, had moved out of New York City and settled in Connecticut. They had met at the Academy and become close friends.

"I'm calling about that art heist that took place over a year ago at Thomas Barkley's home in Connecticut. He's the president of the New London Savings and Loan. He says he knew your father."

Gallery of the Chosen

Ward rubbed the sleep from his eyes. "Yeah, I went to a couple of his parties when I was in college. His son and I went to the same boarding school and then to Princeton."

Tilson continued. "Well, he asked about you and wondered if you would help with this case. We're talking several million dollars' worth of paintings stolen from his house. Anyway, the police have not had much luck breaking the case, so Barkley wants to hire us. But there is something else, something I think you should take a look at. I think there may be a connection between whoever stole his paintings and your wife's murder. I have a photo I want you to see."

Ward's tired mind came alive.

"We're to meet Barkley at his residence in New Canaan at ten o'clock. I'll tell you all about it then. Can you make it?"

"Of course. And you think this could have something to do with Barbara's murder?"

"I'll bet my career on it."

Peter Saunders

Chapter 17: Thomas Barkley

The entrance to Barkley's estate was grand and gated. Cameras peered down from the eight-foot perimeter stone wall and followed Ward's car as it slowly made its way along the winding road up to the huge house. Detective Bob Tilson was sitting in his car waiting for Ward to arrive. He got out as Ward pulled up and together they walked to the front door.

Barkley's residence was a massive chunk of granite. It was a fine example of Georgian architecture with towering columns and high windows. Barkley was waiting for them at the front door and led them across an impressive marble foyer to his elevator. Once upstairs they followed him to his private gallery. Ancient stone carvings stood in glass cases in front of each of the four floor-to-ceiling windows. A dozen paintings hung throughout the gallery, but one wall was bare except for faint outlines of the six stolen paintings. The two detectives sank into deep leather chairs that formed a small semicircle in the center of the enormous gallery.

Barkley, dressed in a pinstriped business suit, moved impatiently back and forth, staring at the outlines of the missing paintings. He walked to a small cabinet that stood against the wall and opened its doors to display a full range of liquors. Pouring a stiff whiskey on ice, he offered the same to his guests. When they declined, Barkley returned to the semicircle and sat down.

"It's good to see you again, Ward. I was troubled to hear about your personal loss. Did they get the bastard?"

Ward shook his head. "Not yet."

Barkley took a deep breath. "That must be very hard on you."

Ward nodded.

Barkley turned his attention to Tilson. "I am late for a meeting, so I'll get right to the point. It's been a little over a year since my paintings were stolen and the police, along with their special units, don't seem to be making any headway in finding whoever took them. Frankly, I have run out of patience." He looked directly at Ward.

"I know with you and Tilson on this case we'll get somewhere. You'll find whoever did this. I don't care what it costs; I want my paintings back and I want whoever did this broken. Do you understand?" Barkley downed the contents of his glass in one gulp. "I'm not interested in insurance money. I want the paintings back, period." Barkley went back to the cabinet and poured himself another drink.

Tilson opened his note pad as Barkley settled back into his chair. "Mr. Barkley, you said you suspected that a friend of your daughter's, a Timothy Stoddard, might be involved?"

"That's correct. Stoddard is the only one outside of the family and our staff who had access to my house. I'm told the alarm system had been professionally disabled, so whoever turned it off, knew where the central control box was and had a key to the room. And Stoddard vanished a couple of days after the robbery. Find this Stoddard character and you'll probably find my paintings."

"We'd like to speak to your daughter," Ward said.

Barkley nodded. "Of course. Right now Katharine is visiting her mother in the South of France. The police have her initial interview on file, but I'll tell her you want to speak with her when she returns in two weeks. I assure you, she'll be more than happy to cooperate."

Tilson looked at his notes. "I did some checking around and here's what I've got on Stoddard. He was a part-time art instructor at NYU. The dean told me that he worked for the university for only half a year. I checked the references listed on his employment application, and they turned out to be bogus. Seems during the interview the Department Chair was so impressed with Stoddard's knowledge of art history, he didn't think he needed to check the guy's credentials. I believe Stoddard took the teaching position so he could meet your daughter. From the description Katharine gave police, they think he was involved in a Denver heist that took place two years ago. His technique was the same. There, he befriended the daughter of a wealthy collector of rare china and worked from the inside, ensuring the thieves a way in and out without detection. He seems to specialize in private collections. Again, he disappeared a few weeks after the robbery took place."

"Any sign of the china?" Barkley asked, a grim expression on his face.

"Not yet. We think he may be working for a larger syndicate overseas."

Barkley slammed his glass down on the oval table positioned between the leather chairs. "I don't give a damn who he's working for. He'll not get away with this, do you hear? No one is going to screw me without paying a price." Barkley's face turned crimson, and his mouth tightened into a nasty snarl. "I want the son-of-a-bitch who stole my paintings found. You understand? Whatever it takes, gentleman, just do it. I want those paintings back. The police have a full description of what was taken with all the identification you'll need. The art houses have been alerted in case he tries to sell them." Barkley stood up and led the detectives back to the front door. He grabbed his coat and departed.

Ward and Tilson watched Barkley drive away in his Mercedes.

"So, how the hell did Stoddard pull this off?" Ward asked. "Barkley isn't someone easily duped."

"Well, first of all, Timothy Stoddard is a fake name. He actually uses several names and has driver's licenses for each. Like Barkley says, Stoddard got to the paintings through his daughter, Katharine. She was the target. She's a dreamy-eyed blueblood with a pedigree that goes way, way back. Daddy is the collector and daughter Katharine is an art major in her final year at NYU. What the thieves were after were six Renaissance paintings. As Barkley indicated, the security cameras and motion detectors had been turned off. Stoddard is our prime suspect. When the police interviewed Katharine, she told them that after about a month of heavy dating, she began sharing Stoddard's apartment on the Westside. She says he told her a bunch of lies about his wealthy British parents being major collectors. Then about two months ago, Katharine brought him home on a weekend to meet daddy and he was given a tour of the gallery. Naturally our boy Timothy was impressed. Barkley may have thought he was meeting a candidate for a son-in-law. After that meeting, Katharine and Timothy often spent weekends here. They had the run of the house when daddy was away on business. The night of the robbery Katharine had let the maid off for the weekend. When Katharine and Timothy returned home from a movie, they found the six paintings gone. Mysteriously the alarm system had been turned off but made to look like someone had forced his or her way into the house. Two weeks later Stoddard went missing."

"So why do you think this case could be connected to Barbara's murder?"

"When Katharine was first interviewed, she was asked how she met Stoddard. They met at a campus event of the athletic club, but she said Stoddard was not athletic at all, never worked out or used the gym. So my guess is that he joined the gym to meet Katharine. She produced a picture of him which I found in the police file." Tilson reached into his pocket and pulled out the photo. "This is Stoddard outside the athletic club on campus." Looking straight at the camera, Stoddard, a tall twenty-nine year old, stood with his arm around Katharine's shoulder. He wore a grey, nylon sweat suit. Printed across the front jacket was an image of a large red beetle with the word Scarab printed beneath. Tilson looked at Ward, "The jacket Stoddard's wearing matches the jacket worn by the man seen in the surveillance video taken at the auto rental. Whoever stole the van used in your wife's murder wore a similar jacket."

Chapter 18: Elizabeth's Diaries

A few days later, Ward had received a call from Susan begging to meet. Normally he didn't mix his home life with his office visits, but since Susan could only come early in the morning, Ward agreed to meet with her at his apartment. At 8 a.m. the downstairs buzzer rang and a few minutes later there was a knock at the door.

"Come in, come in," Ward said as he took her coat and led her into his living room. "Can I get you something to drink?"

"Juice would be fine, thanks," Susan said as she settled into a chair. Looking up she saw the posters lining Ward's living room wall.

Ward grabbed the juice container from the fridge along with two glasses and seated himself in the winged backed chair facing Susan. As he poured the juice and handed her a glass, he was startled at the noticeable change in her appearance. Susan looked fragile. Her shoulders were slightly hunched over, her hair in need of brushing.

She stared at photos pinned to the right-hand corner of each poster board. "May I ask who the women in the photos are?"

"Those women were murdered the same way my wife was murdered."

"Is your wife's picture up there?"

"Ward pointed to the picture on the last poster board. "That's Barbara."

"Why do you have their pictures posted on your wall? I'm sorry, it's none of my business."

"No need to apologize. I am collecting information on each victim, looking for similarities in their circumstances and profiles. It helps if I can see the details of each woman's life and compare them. I have a hunch one person may have killed all of them, but it's still only a hunch. The photos remind me these were real people, not just names in a police report."

Susan took a deep breath. "You mean none of these women's murderers have been captured?"

"I'm afraid not and that suggests we may be looking for one person. Whoever killed them is still out there, free to take more lives."

"That's horrible."

Ward looked at his wife's photo then continued. "Bull and I are making headway in your grandmother's case. I think we may have found something."

Susan interrupted. "That's why I'm here. I'm getting pretty nervous about the whole thing. Two days ago someone broke into my grandmother's house when I was at work and searched it. I came home around 5:30 and found the door had been forced open."

"Was anything taken?"

"Nothing is missing that I can tell, but the entire house was searched, especially Elisabeth's bedroom and the basement."

"Are valuables kept at the house?"

"No, no money or jewelry. But I have a feeling the person was looking for my grandmother's diaries because whoever broke in spent a great deal of time in the basement looking through her trunks."

Ward's back stiffened. "Your grandmother kept diaries?"

"She kept them from the time she moved to Seawood. They were locked in a trunk in the basement."

"Why didn't the thieves take the trunk?"

"They didn't have a chance. The trunk and the diaries were in my car. Elizabeth told me the day before she died where the diaries were and asked that I hide them."

"Did you ask her why?"

"Yes. She said she wanted me to have them and she was afraid her brother or my mother would throw them out. She said I would need them, but that's all she said."

"Are they still in your car?"

"No, my boyfriend has them in his apartment."

"Good, leave them there. Do you think they go back to when your grandmother was first married?"

"Could be. There are a lot of them, but I would have to check."

"Does the name Johnny Lynks mean anything to you?"

Susan thought for a moment and then shook her head. "No, I don't think I've heard that name before. Who is he?"

"He lived in Seawood before your mother was born and apparently knew your grandmother and grandfather. Your grandmother never mentioned him?"

"No, I'm sure she didn't."

"Johnny Lynks may help us find the answers you're looking for. Can you get me those diaries?"

Susan hesitated before responding. "I'm sorry, but I wouldn't feel comfortable sharing Elizabeth's private thoughts with strangers."

Ward nodded. "I understand. Will you look through them? Check around the time your grandmother moved to Seawood, right up to the time your mother was born and see if the name Johnny Lynks shows up?"

Susan put her glass down and leaned forward. "I'm getting the feeling something terribly wrong happened."

"Why do you say that?"

"When my mother called that evening and yelled at me for contacting you, she was pretty angry but there was something else in her voice I haven't heard before. My mother has always been the cool one. But that evening she actually sounded frightened. Do you have any idea why my mother might be frightened?"

"I'm not sure, but if there's something she doesn't want uncovered and you sense her nervousness, we must be close to finding answers."

Susan looked away then turned back. "I suppose this is what you meant when you said that maybe I should let sleeping dogs lie?"

Ward nodded.

Susan looked at the poster boards across the room and the photos of the murdered women. "I wish I could help you find whoever murdered those women." She stood to leave. "I'll look through the diaries for the name Johnny Lynks."

Peter Saunders

Chapter 19: The Letter

In early spring, the Ward and Bull reviewed where their investigations stood. They were working on the search for Barbara's murderer, the Dwyer case, and their hunt for Timothy Stoddard. Clearly Stoddard was involved in the theft of Barkley's paintings, and now there was a possibility he might somehow be involved with Barbara's murder. Bull insisted on sticking with the Dwyer case and their search for Johnny Lynks. Ward admired Bull's determination and courage, but he cautioned his partner that things could get nasty, especially if one of the mafia families took objection to their investigation.

Ward was following up on leads Professor Rapin had given him when Bull called late one morning with news he had found an old fisherman at Seawood who remembered someone named Lynks. Bull also had some personal news he wanted to share. They agreed to meet at Nick's for lunch. At noon, Ward grabbed his mail and drove out to Nick's Seafood Shack.

To those in the know, Nick's was the only hamburger and clam joint in town! The McDonald's up on Main Street was for tourists. Nick's was for locals and those from the Big Apple in the know. The aroma of onions and burgers frying on the open pit would turn a vegetarian into a raging carnivore. The little neck clams never disappointed. The early warmth of spring made it a perfect day to sit outside. Ward ordered the usual for both of them. As he took a seat at one of the umbrella covered picnic tables, he glanced quickly through the mail. A letter from a Mr. John Tucker, P.C., Attorney, Queens, New York, caught his attention. Ward set the letter aside as the guy behind the counter delivered Ward's order.

Bull arrived carrying travel magazines under his arm. A wide grin spread across his face as he examined the food and sat down. "Thanks for lunch, Boss." He flipped open one of the magazines, stopping at an article on the single women of Brazil.

"Listen to this. The guy who wrote this article says the single women in Brazil love American men. There are three women for each man. The beautiful women of Brazil will actually grab your butt to get your attention and are not shy about physically fighting each other for a guy they like."

The look in Bull's eyes suggested he was imagining just such a fight now.

"Is this the exciting news you mentioned?"

Bull nodded as he went to work on his lunch.

"That's terrific," Ward said and then tried to change the subject. He filled Bull in on Susan's visit and the revelation of her grandmother's diaries. But Bull was too absorbed by the pictures of the babes in thongs parading across the Brazilian beaches to focus on what Ward was saying.

"Hello, Ward to Ranger Bull. Are you receiving?"

Bull brushed aside Ward's attempts to divert his attention. "Hey, come on, this is important. It says a guy can meet two or more women in a single day." Bull's mouth dropped open when he caught sight of one woman stretched out across the entire next page. Ward stuck a fry in Bull's mouth and pushed it shut.

"Save your energy. You'll need it if you're going to take on the women of Brazil. Tell me what turned up on Lynks."

Bull chewed his fry and swallowed it, but he didn't take his eyes off the lovely tan female smiling up from the page. "Oh, yeah. Lynks." He took one last look, folded the corner of the page down neatly and closed the magazine. He reached for his note pad. "I finally found someone who's heard of Lynks. There's an old geezer living out by the Navy Yard who thinks he remembers a young Lynks in his twenties. This Lynks worked on the docks and around Seawood for a few years at odd jobs. He claims Lynks was a charmer, a sweet guy always willing to help. Seems the local ladies liked him too. The guy didn't know where Lynks came from or where he went. One day he just ups and disappears."

"Did Lynks work on the Dwyer fishing boat?"

"No, but he did work on a competing boat, the Clipper. He worked as a deckhand cleaning fish, rigging poles and scrubbing the deck at the end of each day."

"Did your contact remember anything else?"

"Well, I mentioned the battle for dock space, but the guy claimed he didn't know anything about that."

"So, Lynks was a nice guy, liked by all? That's it?"

A bird landed on the edge of their table and eyed the fries. Ward tossed one on the ground and the bird followed.

"No, not everyone liked Lynks. He would frequent the local tavern and the old guy remembers a fight one night between Lynks and Elizabeth's husband, Todd. He says Todd warned Lynks not to come near his family or his boat again."

"Did this guy say why Todd threatened Lynks?"

"Nope, but he did say that people thought Todd was nuts because Lynks would never have harmed a fly. Lynks was the darling of the bay. And by the way, it seems the Dwyer family had quite a reputation."

"What kind of a reputation?"

Bull downed the last morsel of his burger and wiped his mouth with the napkin. "All he would say was that the Dwyer boys were wild growing up and into all sorts of trouble. Oh, yeah, get this; rumor had it that the family and the boat were cursed."

"Really? Just what we need, a curse."

"Curse, with a capital C. Isn't that cool! This case is getting better by the day. A mysterious body in a grave, along with a cursed family and boat. It sounds like a Stephen King novel."

"So, what made this guy think the family was cursed?"

"Well, first brother Pete falls overboard and drowns, and then Elizabeth's husband, Todd, dies of a heart attack. Then Ed dies mysteriously and just in case you still don't buy the curse idea, brother Al ends up a raging alcoholic more than a little off his rocker and is sent away. And when Lynks disappeared never to return, that really spooked the locals and hurt the Dwyer fishing business. The only ones willing to go on their boat were customers from somewhere else. The old guy claims Elizabeth and her younger brother Paul were the only sane members of the family. People believed the curse began when Elizabeth's mother died, then all hell broke loose and things went from bad to worse. Some locals even blamed the curse for all the bad fishing in the area. Local boats made sure they left plenty of ocean between themselves and the Dwyer boat. Of course, none of this rules out the possibility that Lynks might have been murdered."

"Well, we're not sure Lynks was murdered, and we're not sure the Dwyers did it if he was. We need a motive," Ward added.

Bull put his food down. "Suppose one of the mafia families killed Lynks to protect their interests, and the Dwyers agreed to bury him so no one would know where he went. That old geezer told me Lynks just up and left Seawood without a word to anyone and didn't even take any of his possessions. There were all kinds of rumors floating around, but after a year or so people moved on to other things. Problem is none of this explains why both the Gerberti and Agrelo clans supported the Dwyers in their bid to win back their dock space."

Ward nodded. "We're assuming that Lynks was somehow involved with both the Dwyer family and one of the Mafia families and together they murdered him and buried him in Dwyer's family plot. I'm sure Uncle Paul and probably Angela know Lynks is in the grave and they're worried we will find him as we work on Susan's case."

Bull wrinkled his forehead, indicating he wasn't convinced. "So why would they want Lynks killed? As to who could have killed him, Todd and brothers Pete and Ed died before Lynks disappeared, so it was either Al, who was incapable of doing anything other than drink, or Paul who was only sixteen. Still, he could have done it. Of course, it could have been Elizabeth, but from what Susan told you, that would be a long shot. Then again, sharing a grave with someone you murdered wouldn't be much fun. She did ask her granddaughter to forgive her. So maybe she did do it."

"I doubt that Elizabeth was a murderer. But a member of the Gerberti family or one of their goons could have helped them out with the Dwyers agreeing to bury Lynks. We need a motive. Without that, we are going nowhere."

Bull scratched his head. "What about the cries Bertini heard? Whose cries were they?"

"Bertini could have heard Lynks crying for help, but we still need proof Lynks was murdered. Elizabeth's diaries may provide that proof."

Bull sat back and shook his head. "Even if we could prove that Lynks was murdered, pinning it on anyone would be next to impossible unless Elizabeth actually fingered the murderer in her diary. And what's the point? I mean most of the people involved are dead. And suppose Susan drops the whole thing? This seems a whole lot more complicated than it did when we started. I wonder if it's worth all the effort?"

Ward took hold of Bull's hand just as he was about to down another fry. "If the Gerberti family was responsible for the murder of my wife, or if they know who is responsible and our nailing the Dwyer family helps me get to them, then this will be worth all our effort. Don't you agree?" Ward released Bull's arm.

"Hey, I forgot to show you my summer regimen." Bull pulled a six-month calendar from among his magazines and pushed it under Ward's nose for inspection. Bull had divided his summer weeks into an impressive regime of exercise schedules with times each week devoted to building up different parts of his body. He flipped through a few weeks and explained how his plan would work. Shoving a few more fries into his mouth, he stood up to emphasize the extent of his impending transformation. "Man, when I get through with this routine, I'm going to have a real body—powerful arms, a v-shaped back, wash-board abs, tight butt and muscular legs." Bull held up a magazine picture of a well-built athlete.

He pulled his pant leg up and shoved his hairy log of a leg out for inspection. "No more of these chubby tree trunks I'm walking around on. The Brazilian women are going to go nuts when they catch sight of me. My ass will be covered with so many pinch marks, I may need a bodyguard."

Ward smiled, "I have one question?"

"What's that?"

"Well, I'm no expert, but it seems to me your diet needs a plan as well as your body. I mean fries, hamburgers, buttered corn, and soft drinks? Think of all the sugar and calories. My guess is that you will have to curb your appetite for sweets and all the fatty foods, and then lose at least fifty pounds to start off with if you want to look like that guy." Ward pointed to the picture.

It was clear from the look on Bull's face that he didn't like what he was hearing. "That's going to be rough, isn't it?"

Ward nodded and pulled Bull's plate in his direction, then started eating the remaining fries. Bull stared at the plate as it retreated from under his nose and watched the fries disappear, one by one.

"Maybe I should go slowly, you know, not rush the program."

The corners of Ward's mouth turned up in a slight smile. "You mean kind of sneak up on the diet thing?"

"That's it. Sneak up on it." Bull retrieved the plate.

Ward turned his attention to the letter from John Tucker, the attorney. He had written to inform Ward that his firm represented both the Dwyer and the King family interests. Uncle Paul and Angela were deeply concerned about Susan's health since Susan's grandmother had passed away. The families were convinced that the stress of her grandmother's passing had been too much for Susan, and they feared it would eventually lead to a nervous breakdown unless actions were taken to assist her.

Mr. Tucker drew Ward's attention to the fact that the family doctor had brought this to their attention and suggested the family do everything within its power to help Susan.

Mr. Tucker had been instructed to request that Ward remove himself from Miss King's services in the interest of her health. The family would compensate him for any expenses incurred to date. He was to fax his bill or visit Mr. Tucker's office in Queens at his earliest convenience.

Bull had finished revising his exercise program. "Anything good?" he asked peeking at the name on the envelope.

Ward read him the contents.

"Well, we sure got their attention, didn't we? So what are you going to do?"

"Play along. I need to stall them till Susan has had a look at the diaries." Ward went to the public telephone and dialed Tucker's number. Someone picked up.

"Hello, this is Ward Emerson. Please connect me with Mr. Tucker."

"Just a moment, please."

Gallery of the Chosen

Tucker immediately picked up his phone. "Mr. Emerson, I'm glad you called. The Dwyer and King families appreciate your full cooperation. I'm sure you share their concern about Susan's health. They need your assistance to ensure that her recovery is not jeopardized. If you have any expenses we will take care of them…"

Ward cut him off. "What I have are a number of questions I would like cleared up before I agree to drop this case." The silence on the other end suggested that Tucker didn't like Ward's approach.

"Mr. Emerson, there is no case. We don't know what you're referring to. If you have expenses the Dwyer family is prepared to reimburse you for your work."

"What I would like are answers to my questions."

"What kind of questions?" Tucker's pleasant tone sounded strained.

"Interesting questions, but I think I'll save those till we meet face to face."

Tucker put him through to his secretary. Ward could hear Tucker instructing her to clear his calendar. Ward pretended to be tied up all next week to give Susan time to search the diaries. They finally set a date and Ward hung up.

Bull had finished scanning another article and looked up. "So, what's next?"

"Well, our best hope is the diaries. I want you to see if you can dig up anything on Tucker. Give Rapin a call and see if Tucker has any connections to organized crime, especially the Gerberti family. After I hear from Susan, I'll visit Mr. Tucker."

Peter Saunders

Chapter 20: The Elusive Mr. Tucker, P.C.

Located about a mile from the ocean sat a stone building surrounded by gardens. It was Tucker's Valley Stream office. Tucker's secretary was busy watching a popular soap on a small TV when Ward arrived. Although she turned the volume down as Ward approached her desk, she had trouble keeping her eyes off the screen. Not wanting to compete with *General Hospital*, Ward tilted his head toward the television and cleared his throat. The secretary glanced briefly at the TV and reluctantly turned it off.

"I'm Ward Emerson."

The secretary had no sooner alerted Tucker of Ward's arrival, when Tucker's door flew open and the man himself strode into the room. He was in his sixties, but his grey Armani suit, powder blue silk shirt and pale yellow tie gave him a more youthful appearance. Bull would have been jealous!

Tucker was tall and thin. There was a measured fluidity in Tucker's movements, all intended to impress. Everything about him seemed practiced, as if he were playing a character in a melodrama. The real Tucker was nowhere to be seen. When he spoke, one could hear the collection of sounds all calculated to suggest decisiveness and strength. Tucker shot his hand out and pumped Ward's arm as if he were a politician stumping for votes.

Ward had come across Tucker's type before and knew he was as phony as the doctors on the soaps. Behind their façades lay ruthless, cunning manipulators, unburdened by rules of ethics or morals. The Tuckers of the world floated along without compunction or restraints. They preyed on those encumbered by such rules. The successful Tuckers had learned to mimic society's values as a mirror reflects the image before it.

"Mr. Emerson, it's a pleasure to meet you. Please come in."

Tucker's private office was meant to impress, to fool the eye and inspire awe and confidence. The oversized furniture was a blend of leather, metal and glass, all perfectly balanced, all carefully positioned to enclose those who happened to find themselves in Tucker's trap.

Like a spider, Tucker had spun his web and waited. But when looking more closely, one realized that everything was an imitation meant to fool the eye. Even the rows of legal tomes lining the impressive bookcase were nothing more than hollow pieces of wood shaped to look like books.

In the center of the room was a thick carpet on which sat a coffee table and four high-backed chairs. A large mirror hung on the wall and looked down on the chairs and table. A side door suggested there was another room somewhere in the back. Across the room was a large picture window that looked out on one of the gardens surrounding Tucker's building.

Ward could not help but think of Rapin's stinking little office buried in the basement.

Tucker escorted Ward to one of the chairs and took the opposite one. "I've done a little research on you, Mr. Emerson. I always like to know the measure of the man or woman I'm dealing with. You have quite a reputation. Yes sir, quite a reputation. It is truly an honor to have someone of your caliber visit my humble office. Let me get right to the point. My clients are very concerned about Susan King's emotional state, and they need your cooperation." Tucker gracefully crossed his legs and brought his hands together with a flourish as if he was about to pray. "I understand you wish clarification on some minor points. I will do my best to provide the information you need so we can both move on to other, more important, productive issues."

Ward decided to play Tucker's game. "Well now, John," Ward said after clearing his throat. "My client wants to know why her family is so jumpy about her grandmother's final request. And to tell the truth, I'm kind of curious myself."

"Good, good. No circling around an issue. No wasting time. I like that approach." Tucker's face formed a grotesque smile that reminded Ward of the evil Joker character in the Batman comics. "Susan has a history of, shall we say, imaging things. Her family has grown accustomed to her fantasies and manic swings from euphoria to doubt and depression. She is by nature suspicious like her grandmother."

"So, you think Susan imagined that her grandmother wished to be buried separately?" Ward studied Tucker's reaction as his smile vanished.

Gallery of the Chosen

"Don't put words in my mouth. I did not say that. As you well know, we can only go on the evidence we have and the advice of the family doctor. Susan's mother and uncle believe Elizabeth was confused when she made that request. They understand why Susan is reluctant to accept the state of her grandmother's mind, but the fact remains, Elizabeth was delirious. The real issue is how we can help Susan get a better grasp of reality and control of her emotions." Tucker paused briefly and then continued. "The sad truth is that Elizabeth was paranoid all her life, thinking that someone was out to harm her and her family. You can imagine the impact that must have had on her daughter, Angela, and her grandchild, Susan. It was especially hard on Susan who now suffers from the same condition and who trusted Elizabeth implicitly. However, it was only natural Elizabeth's family refused to give into such obsessive fears regarding her final resting place. Unfortunately, Susan came to believe her mother and uncle were conspiring against Elizabeth. It is sad, truly sad."

"Do you mean Elizabeth believed they wished to harm her?"

"Well, not directly, but harm her nevertheless by refusing to live in her reality. I am told such fears are not unusual for patients with Elizabeth's condition and it is clear Susan shared some of these fears. The family doctor can document all of this, but he would need Susan's permission to share such information."

"Did Elizabeth ever consult with a psychiatrist?"

"I can tell you that her doctor advised her to see a psychiatrist, but I'm told Elizabeth was old fashioned. She was of that generation that believed only patients with severe mental illnesses sought psychiatric help. No, Elizabeth trusted her family doctor and no one else. What greatly concerns the family is that Susan's delusions will only get worse if we support her fears." Tucker glanced at his watch. "Are there any other points, I can clarify for you, Ward?"

"Yes, Susan claims that her Uncle Paul threatened her."

A half smile appeared on Tucker's face. "Well, as I have indicated to you, Susan shares her grandmother's tendency to see enemies where there aren't any. Paul Dwyer is her godfather and loves her very much. He has tried repeatedly to shake her out of her mistaken notions. Sometimes he loses patience with her, which is understandable, but he would never threaten her. I suspect he may have scolded her but threaten her? That is very unlikely."

It was clear that Tucker was pleased with the way he was controlling things, so Ward decided it was time to throw him a curve. Ward abruptly stood up and headed for the door, then paused. "Well, you have been very helpful, John. Very helpful."

Tucker looked up somewhat perplexed by Ward's sudden departure. "I'm pleased you have an open mind. Susan is a lovely girl, and I know you would not want to hurt her. If you tell me how much we owe you…" He moved to his desk and removed a checkbook from a drawer.

"Nothing!"

Tucker's head snapped up. He fixed Ward with a disappointed expression. "Nothing? That's very generous, very generous indeed, but surely there are some incidentals we can take care of?"

Ward opened the door, and then turned back briefly "No, John, but I will verify what you have said."

Tucker seemed relieved. "Oh, by all means. Call Paul Dwyer or Angela King. I will tell them to expect your call."

"Thanks, John, I'll do that." Ward walked into the hallway, waited a few minutes and then poked his head back into Tucker's office.

"Have you ever wondered what Elizabeth was frightened of down in the family grave? I've been giving that some thought."

Tucker's face went white. Ward left him speechless—something Tucker had not experienced very often.

A few moments after Ward left, the door inside Tucker's office opened. A well-dressed, grey haired man, leaning on a cane, moved slowly across the room and sat with some difficulty in one the chairs. His glasses were as thick as coke bottles. He sat erect with his eyes closed.

Tucker studied the man's worried expression. "He must be bluffing. He couldn't possibly know," Tucker said.

The elderly man opened his eyes. "You're wrong, John. He knows."

Tucker moved to the opposite chair. "We did it Paul's way, Rafael, but as I told you before, I don't believe this Ward Emerson is an ordinary detective. He will need something tangible to get his attention."

"You know how Paul and I feel about this."

Gallery of the Chosen

Tucker leaned slightly forward and made eye contact. He lowered his voice. "This situation is serious. The family does not want this issue to surface. We need to send Mr. Emerson and his partner a clear message." Tucker pointed to the large mirror on the wall. "You saw him and heard him; money won't work."

Rafael shifted uneasily in his chair. "I don't want Antonio involved in this. We agreed."

Tucker lowered his head in frustration, and then raised it again. "I know, but if we don't get this detective to back off, your nephew will take over. You know how Antonio likes to take care of things. Let me try. Emerson will not get hurt, I promise. We'll just send him a message."

Rafael looked long and hard at Tucker as if seeking some alternative.

Tucker waited patiently, but finally forced the issue. "Rafael, we've discussed this matter before. The only way is to go forward."

Rafael looked back at Tucker and slowly nodded his consent.

Peter Saunders

Chapter 21: Message Received

At *The Standard Star* newspaper office, a group of reporters stood at the water cooler outside of Bull's cramped and stuffy cubical. They were swapping stories about the newspaper's new VP; a man they all agreed was a creep. Bull had learned to tune out such conversations. As the new kid at the office, the VP wouldn't even know he existed and that suited Bull just fine. Vincent Toolman was on his way to becoming a first class detective trained by Ward Emerson, one of the city's best. Even when the summers were brutal, the fact that his cubical was at the furthest corner from any open window didn't bother Bull now. His dull life stuck in cramped and sweaty cubicles would soon be history.

Bull scanned the travel brochures spread out before him, peering intensely at the photos of a raft climbing and then descending a wall of white water. In the next two photos, the raft emerged successfully and raced down Oregon's mighty Rogue River. *My life is boring now.* Bull looked longingly at the photos. *What I need are experiences that test my mettle, like white water rafting.*

His eyebrows suddenly formed a furrow. How would his generous body fit into those restrictive wetsuits? How could he breathe? He peered at another photo of rafters battling the rapids. It was impossible to see through the torrents of water whether anyone matched his bulk. Diet alone would not produce the kind of body he would need to tackle a river like the Rogue. He wondered what sizes wetsuits came in and what colors.

"Toolman?" An elderly man pushing a mail cart came shuffling past. "You got mail, Sonny." The letter he tossed landed on Bull's desk. "Two points," the man said, pushing his cart onto the next cubicle.

Bull picked up the envelope. It had no return name or address. Inside was a single sheet of paper with driving directions to a Jones Beach parking lot out on Long Island. Two short sentences instructed Bull to call the listed phone number if he wanted information on Johnny Lynks. The letter bore the initials W.C.

W.C.? Who the hell is W.C.? Bull dialed the number and waited.

"Hello."

"This is Vincent Toolman calling. I just received your letter."

"Mr. Toolman? This is Wilbur Cousins." The man's voice faded briefly.

"Who?" Bull asked. "Who?"

"Wilbur Cousins, the fellow at the Navy Yard outside of Seawood. Remember?"

Bull pushed the brochures aside so he could concentrate. "Wilbur?" Suddenly he made the connection. "Of course I remember you. You say you have more information on Johnny Lynks?"

"Well, after you left I asked around. Anyway, a friend calls me the other night and says there's a guy out here with information you would be real interested in."

Bull reached for his notepad. "What kind of information?"

"Well, I can't say for sure, but if you're willing to pay good money, this guy says he's got all kinds of information on Lynks."

"Who is this person? Can you tell me his name and phone number?"

"Like I've been telling you, this fellow is not someone I know personally. And I'm told he will only talk to you face to face." Wilbur cleared his throat twice. "Listen Mr. Toolman, I'm none too comfortable doing this, and I don't want to get involved any more than I have to. I'm sure you understand. You got the directions, right?"

"I have them right here."

Wilbur's voice trembled a little. "Good. So, here's what the fellow said."

Bull was puzzled by Wilbur's nervousness, but decided if he probed too much Wilbur would hang up.

"He'll meet you out at the Jones Beach parking lot marked on the map. He'll be there tomorrow at 7 p.m. Bring three hundred dollars with you."

"Why Jones Beach?"

"He didn't say, but that's where he'll be."

"How will I know what this fellow looks like?"

"Just pull into the parking lot and wait. He'll find you. Oh, and he doesn't want you to bring anyone. He was very clear about that. If you bring anyone, the deal is off. Understand?"

"Yes, but I need to know…"

Wilbur had hung up.

"Crazy coot!" Bull tried calling back, but no one answered.

He picked up the receiver and began dialing Ward's number then stopped. *Why am I calling Ward? Wilbur says I can't bring anyone so there's no use calling Ward. He'll want to go. Besides, I know I can pull this off on my own.* Bull smiled. *Won't Ward be surprised when I lay Lynks' whole story on him?*

Bull had trouble finding the isolated parking lot near Jones Beach and was already thirty minutes late. The dirt road threw up a cloud of dust as his car turned a corner. Ahead was a sign indicating this was the right parking lot. Bull pulled in and slowed his car to a crawl. There was one other car, a Lincoln Continental. It was parked at the far end of the lot and appeared to be empty. Bull drove toward the Lincoln but decided to stop half way. He turned off the engine and got out. His armpits, neck and back were sweaty and his back was stiff from the long drive. He pulled the shirt away from his skin and turned from side to side letting the ocean breezes cool him. Sounds of ocean waves breaking against the shore were clear, but eight foot sand dunes topped with wild grass hid the ocean from view. Terns and gulls circled overhead, protesting his presence. Bull looked around and checked his watch. Then he heard his name being called as a man emerged at the top of a dune some two hundred feet ahead to the left.

"Are you Vincent Toolman?"

"That's me."

The burly figure slowly started down the sandy slope toward him. Bull's heart began racing and for an instant he thought of jumping back in his car, locking the doors and driving away.

"Vincent! I like that name. My brother is a Vincent, too. Small world." When the man reached the bottom of the dune, he paused briefly, and then slowly walked toward the front of Bull's car.

Bull remained standing with the driver's door open, keeping it between him and the approaching hulk.

"Hold it, right there," Bull demanded. *What had he done, coming out here alone? He hadn't told anyone where he was going: not his parents, not Ward, no one. What a stupid rookie mistake.* The approaching man stopped and Bull began to relax. "Wilbur says you have some information on Johnny Lynks that I would be interested in. I have the money you want right here." Bull held up an envelope. "What kind of information do you have?"

"Well, Vince, you see the problem is that Wilbur's mistaken. He's an old man and he gets easily confused. You know how it is. There's nothing worth knowing about Lynks, and we thought we should meet you in person to tell you that so there won't be any future misunderstandings."

"We?" Bull asked.

"Yeah, we." The man smiled, his eyes glancing over Bull's right shoulder.

Bull swung around just in time to catch the full force of a fist in his face.

Chapter 22: Finding Bull

Where the hell's Bull? Ward's repeated phone calls over the past two days went unanswered. Even an invitation to a free lobster dinner didn't work. Ward had checked with the newspaper, Bull's friends and his parents. Ward was about to call the local hospital when he got the call from Brook Norris, Bull's editor at the *Standard Star*.

"We found him!"

"Where the hell is he?"

"He got the shit kicked out of him out on Long Island."

Ward sat down. "What? How bad is he?"

"Not good from what they tell me. I just got off the phone with a Dr. Ahmed. Bull's head and legs are pretty beat up. Someone decided to use him as a punching bag."

Ward's stomach felt sick.

"He's in intensive care and unconscious. I'm heading out there and thought you might want to join me."

Ward's mind was racing. "Which hospital?"

"Brunswick General near Amityville."

"I'll meet you there." Ward hung up and grabbed his jacket.

###

It was 6 p.m. by the time Ward arrived at Brunswick General Hospital. Brook Norris was waiting at the front desk. He had contacted the officer who found Bull and asked if they could meet with him in an hour. Dr. Ahmed was paged. A nurse led Brook and Ward to the ICU section and left the pair standing outside the unit.

"Hello, I'm Dr. Ahmed." The doctor had just come out of surgery and was still wearing his gown and cap.

"I'm Ward Emerson, Mr. Toolman's partner and this is Brook Norris, his employer. How bad is he?"

"Come with me." Dr. Ahmed led them to the narrow X-ray room and snapped on a backlight. They stared at a series of x-rays of Bull's skull and legs. "Mr. Toolman's suffered a cerebral contusion and a fractured leg. The blows to his head have bruised his brain. Whoever did this used his fists and a stick or bat of some sort. There may be some internal bleeding, but we won't know for certain until we do more tests. The next twenty-four hours will be critical. Mr. Toolman has been unconscious since he arrived. You can see him now but only stay a few minutes."

Dr. Ahmed led them to the room where Bull lay unconscious. An oxygen mask covered his nose and mouth and a feeding tube was attached to his arm. His breathing was broken and irregular, his eyelids swollen shut, and what they could see of his face was black and blue and badly swollen. One leg was in a cast and the other wrapped in bandages.

Dr. Ahmed then led them down the hall to the waiting room.

Ward turned to the doctor. "I'm going to be staying at a local motel and will phone in my number. Please have someone call me if there is any change in Vincent's condition."

"Of course, of course, but Mr. Toolman's family should be notified. Can either of you contact them for us?"

Brook jumped in. "Yes, of course. I'll call them."

"Good. Now please excuse me." The doctor left. Not long after, a police officer entered the waiting room.

"I'm Officer Evanski."

While they grabbed coffee from the vending machines and sat down, Norris took care of the introductions.

Ward began. "Can you tell us what happened?"

Officer Evanski nodded. "Mr. Toolman's car was discovered around 9 p.m. in the parking lot of the Tobay Beach. The driver's door was open and from the blood and marks on the ground, we surmised that the victim had been hit from behind with a bat or wooden object. He was then dragged over the sand dunes in the deep weeds and beaten. We believe there were two attackers. The trail of blood made it easy to find Mr. Toolman's body. He must have put up quite a struggle because we found a tooth on the ground nearby." Evanski reached into an envelope he was carrying and pulled out a photo of the tooth.

"A tooth?"

"That's correct. Since Mr. Toolman has all of his own, we believe the tooth belongs to one of his assailants."

Ward smiled at the thought of Bull knocking his attacker's tooth out. It must have been one hell of a punch!

"Would either of you gentlemen have any idea who might have done this?" Evanski asked.

"Vincent and I are private detectives. Vincent is involved in several ongoing investigations, but right off hand I can't help you," Ward said.

Evanski impatiently tapped his pen on his notepad. "This may have been a robbery, but until Mr. Toolman recovers from his head injuries, we won't know for sure why he was there and who met him." Evanski put the photo of the tooth back in the envelope. "Do either of you know why Mr. Toolman was out there?"

"I can tell you he was gathering routine background information. My guess is Vincent made contact with someone he thought might help him."

"What kind of background information? I don't suppose you care to tell me the names of people he was investigating?"

"I really can't give you specific names, but I can tell you that Vincent was looking into the history of privately owned fishing boats and available docking spaces in the Seawood area."

Evanski quickly made a note in his pad. "We believe he intended to meet someone. The parking lot we found him in was pretty remote. Many locals don't even know it exists. The way Mr. Toolman was attacked suggests organized crime had a hand in this. If Mr. Toolman was there for a drug pickup, something went wrong. Do you know if he was involved with drugs?"

Ward shook his head. "No, I can definitely tell you that Vincent was not into drugs and that was not his reason to be at that parking lot. Vincent has never had any connection to organized crime." Ward looked at Norris. "Isn't that so, Norris?"

"Absolutely."

Evanski eyed Ward and Norris closely. "By the way, was Mr. Toolman at a funeral recently?"

Ward and Brook exchanged surprised glances.

"Not to our knowledge. Why do you ask?"

Evanski reached into the envelope again and pulled out another photograph. "We found something in Mr. Toolman's shirt pocket. Does it mean anything to either of you? We're having it checked for fingerprints." He handed the photo to Ward. Brook leaned over to take a look. The photo was a close-up of a sympathy card with the words "Holy Ghost Cemetery" printed across the top. It was the cemetery where the Dwyer family and Lynks were buried. Officer Evanski thanked Ward and Norris and left.

As he departed, Norris turned to Ward. "Why would Bull be carrying a sympathy card in his pocket?"

Ward took a deep breath. "I think it was placed there by his attackers as a message to me."

Chapter 23: Bull's Dream

As Bull lay in a deep sleep, unconscious of visits by his doctors, nurses and friends, he suddenly became aware of a voice calling to him. At first the voice was faint, but it grew louder and more insistent.

"Mr. Toolman! Mr. Toolman!"

I know that voice, Bull thought. It was Susan King calling. "Mr. Toolman, be careful. My mother, Angela, can be very, very persuasive."

Susan's voice faded as Bull was drawn deeper into his dream world, imagining himself back at his apartment. A knock sounded on his front door. He was glad he'd changed his clothes and brushed his teeth when he saw the tall, dreamy-eyed blond with pouting lips standing before him.

"Mr. Toolman?" the shapely woman asked. Her eyes widened as she said Bull's name.

"Yes, I am Vincent Toolman. And you?"

His visitor didn't answer but brushed past him, lightly brushing his cheek with her hand. She made her way to the couch, sat down, leaned back and then crossed her legs. Bull still stood at the door, his jaw slack.

"I would love a drink, Vincent. I've made a long trip from the city and my throat is very dry." She wore a light grey business suit with a skirt that was barely legal. "I'm Angela King, Susan's mother. I believe Susan mentioned me to your boss." There was a long, awkward pause as Angela raised her eyebrows and looked longingly at the liquor bottles on the counter dividing Bull's kitchen from his living room.

Bull slammed the front door and rushed into the kitchen, grabbing the mixing glass and the bottle of gin. "My guess is you're a martini kind of girl," he said.

Angela smiled. "Vincent, how did you know? I would love a martini."

"I am studying to be a detective, remember. You strike me as someone who likes her cocktails strong." Bull smiled his sexiest smile, and congratulated himself on his swift and clever response.

"Yes, a dry martini would be just what I need."

Bull blushed. Sweat began rolling down his broad back as the palms of his hands turned to concrete. How the hell do you make a martini? Is it gin and vermouth or vodka? Guessing, he poured a generous jigger of gin into the mixing glass, added the vermouth and began stirring.

"Olive?" he asked in his best imitation of Humphrey Bogart from the movie Casablanca.

"Two, if you're feeling generous." Angela tossed back her head and Bull stared at her long, blond hair, as it seemed to dance from side to side in graceful swirls. He lost count of the olives and briefly considered making a martini for himself, but decided it was too risky. Instead he poured water into his martini glass and added two olives. He hoped Angela didn't notice the slight shaking of his hand as he delivered her drink and sat across from her, trying not to stare at her gorgeous attributes. It took all the concentration he could muster just to keep breathing.

Angela took a sip and closed her eyes. "Oh, this is a very good martini, Vincent."

Bull felt exhilarated. Situations such as these took a special kind of skill, the kind he knew he possessed. He could hardly wait to tell Ward and the guys at the newspaper office about his encounter with the mysterious Angela. He took a deep breath and tightened his stomach muscles. "I'm delighted you like my martinis. Now then, what can I do for you?"

Angela smiled but said nothing. She began rubbing the lip of her martini glass gently with her index finger. Her finger went around several times and then reversed directions before she took another sip. "I can see you are very, very good at what you do, Vincent."

Bull's head felt heavy. Was it possible Angela was putting him into a trance?

Angela was not to be rushed, and Bull was happy to oblige. He could tell she knew her way around men. Bull sucked his stomach in even tighter; glad he had spent an extra five minutes lifting weights that morning. He could feel the difference throughout his body.

"I have come to make you a proposition." Angela smiled and blinked her bedroom eyes at him, then coyly patted the cushion next to her. "Come sit by me, Vincent. I'm feeling vulnerable."

Bull felt an enormous lump forming in his throat. He could barely swallow and raised his glass to take another sip, surprised when he discovered the glass was empty. The back of his shirt was definitely damp. He tried to speak but could only produce a high-pitched squeak.

"Please, Vincent. Come sit next to me. You are not going to make me beg, are you?"

Bull prayed his deodorant was working as he settled beside Angela, his shirt now soaked.

"Has my wretched daughter told lies about me?" Bull couldn't think of anything to say. "She has made my life miserable. I can tell you are a sensitive, understanding man who shows lots of courage. I heard how you knocked that brute's tooth out. Yes, you are the kind of man women look for." Angela reached over and laid her hand on his knee.

Bull thought he felt clouds of steam rising from his collar. Could the human body actually produce steam? Was it physically possible? Would Angela notice? Would she even care?

"Bull, Bull?"

Angela's voice now seemed to come from far away, yet she leaned over and kissed him squarely on the lips. He could feel her soft breasts pressed firmly against his chest. Bogart would be proud of him.

"Bull? Can you hear me?"

Who was calling? Why wouldn't they leave him alone, and let him enjoy this moment with a woman of the world? In an act of pure passion, Bull took Angela in his arms, concentrating on the feel of her flesh. Angela's body slowly succumbed to his embrace.

"Bull, can you hear me? Are you in pain?" The voice was close, but it was a man's voice.

Bull blinked and slowly opened his eyes, turning toward the speaker.

Angela's voluptuous body had disappeared. Instead, sitting at the side of the bed was Ward.

Peter Saunders

Chapter 24: The Lonely Night

The next day, the doctor told Ward that the swelling in Bull's brain was subsiding and, although Bull had regained consciousness, it was better for him to sleep as it would speed up his recovery. Still, Ward felt helpless and spent his time pacing the hospital halls. After Barbara's death, Bull had become an anchor in Ward's life. The beating he received and the sympathy card in his pocket were warnings that Ward should back off from his investigation of the Dwyer family and Johnny Lynks.

As Ward made his way back to the hospital waiting room, he spotted Bull's father and mother at the reception desk. They had driven down as soon as they were notified that Bull was beaten up. Each day they would drive in, stay for a few hours, and then head back home. Ward avoided them whenever he could. Now in their late seventies, Bruce and Mildred Toolman looked tired. They had never wanted their son to become a detective. When Bruce spotted Ward, he marched over to him.

"Who did this? Who would want to beat up my son?" Bruce glared at Ward, challenging him.

"I'm not sure, but I promise I'll find out. You have my word."

"Your word?" The muscles on Bruce's face tightened, his eyes filled with anger. "You're the reason my son is in this condition."

"Bruce!" Mildred took hold of her husband's arm, trying to calm him, but he pushed her hand away.

"No, Mildred. He needs to hear what I have to say. We've been patient with Vincent. We warned him about this line of work." Bruce pointed at Ward. "If it weren't for you, he might have moved up at the newspaper, instead of wasting his life on some crazy idea of becoming a detective. It was you who put that idea in his head. He sure as hell would not be lying in a hospital all smashed up if he still worked for the newspaper. And you talk about finding out who did this. If you want to help, leave our son alone; find someone else to do your dirty work. That's how you can help my family." Bruce stormed off down the hall.

"He didn't mean that," Mildred said. "He's just upset." She turned and followed after her husband.

I have to get out of here, Ward whispered to himself. He stopped at the reception desk to make sure the hospital had his motel phone number. Again, he instructed them to call him if there was any change in Bull's condition. Then he called Michelle. She would be performing at the tavern, but for the first time he felt the need to reach out to her the way he had reached out to Barbara. He left the name and phone number of his motel on her machine, but before he hung up he added, "I need you. Come if you can."

Minutes later, Ward reached his motel. The cool air felt good as he walked down to the beach and sat on the cold sand. There was no moon to show where sea and sky met, only darkness. Ward stretched out on the sand and closed his eyes.

Exhaustion and the sting of Bruce's criticism had sapped what little energy Ward had left. What could he say? Bruce was right. Maybe Bull would've been better off if he had never met Ward or if Ward had refused to take Bull on as a partner. Had he miscalculated the Dwyer case completely? He was pretty sure he had hit a nerve with those who knew that Lynks was buried in the Dwyer plot, but he hadn't anticipated them hurting Bull. Ward stared up at the dark sky until sleep finally took hold.

"Ward! Ward!" Michelle's voice brought him back to consciousness. He glanced toward the motel and could see her silhouette against its neon sign.

"Ward!" she called again.

"Down here, Michelle. This way." He kept talking, guiding her in the direction of his voice. A moment later, Ward and Michelle embraced.

###

At 10 a.m. the next morning, Bull was moved from intensive care into a private room. The doctor assured everyone that his patient would make a full recovery. At 5 p.m. Bull's parents headed back home. Ward and Michelle waited to get the doctor's report on Bull's recovery and were in the hospital cafeteria when a young man approached their table.

"Are you Ward Emerson?"

Ward nodded, raising an eyebrow at the young man's extraordinary outfit. He wore a bright aquamarine, neoprene surfer's suit under a much wrinkled sports jacket and baggy pants.

"Can I snag a few minutes of your time? I'm Ben Getty, Amityville's kick-ass reporter. I'm a friend of Bull's."

Ward smiled and motioned Ben to take a seat. His sun-dyed blond hair, tan skin and blue shaded Bolle glasses created the impression that his pupils were floating in cool pools of water. His jacket and pants were damp.

"Have you been surfing?" Michelle asked, amused by his attire.

"Right on. Anytime I can get aerial, I will."

Michelle and Ward exchanged a questioning glance. "Arial?"

"Yeah, I'm no grom, no weekender kook."

Ward gave up trying to translate. "You wanted to see me?"

"Right. I met Bull when he was out here a couple of weeks ago. He's rickt, and was pumped about our rendezvous with the mother of all rapids in Oregon. I just wanted you to know if there is anything I can do, I'm on it."

"Do you have any idea who could have attacked him?"

Ben shook his head. "Negative, but from what the local fuzz say, Bull put himself right in the zone!"

"The zone?"

"Yeah, once you are in the zone, there's no escaping the wave's wrath. Bull was in the zone. He hit a real wall."

"I see. Well, Ben, if I think of anything, where can I contact you?"

When Ben stood up, sand fell from his hair on to the table. He looked around for something to write with as he grabbed a paper napkin. Ward offered his pen.

"Right on. Bull will be vertical again. He's no sponger. He'll hold on and land it."

Ben wrote his telephone number, waved, then walked away. Michelle and Ward exchanged smiles as they watched him disappear through the doors. "I had no idea Bull had such eclectic friends," Michelle said.

"Neither did I. You know I tried to dissuade Bull from following this career. But he was determined and it turns out he's becoming a fine detective. I'm lucky to have him as a partner. He helped me, just as you helped me when I needed it the most. I'm forever grateful to you both."

Michelle leaned across the table and kissed Ward on the cheek. "Unfortunately I have to head back to New Rochelle, but I'd like you to call me if there's any change in Bull's condition." She stood and gathered her jacket. "I'll call you tonight at your motel. Are you going to be okay?"

Ward nodded and walked Michelle to her car. He took her into his arms.

"You'll call me as soon as Bull wakes up?" Michelle insisted.

"I promise."

As she drove away, Ward noticed a white Mercedes pulling into the lot and parking in one of the handicapped spots near the hospital door. The driver, a tall blond, stepped out and removed a basket of flowers from the trunk. She was dressed in a grey business suit. The elderly man in the passenger seat stayed in the car.

Ward went back to Bull's room. More color had returned to his face, and he seemed to be sleeping more peacefully. Ward checked his watch. In half an hour, Dr. Ahmed would make his rounds and Ward wanted to be present for that.

I can use a cup of coffee, he thought as he headed for the vending machine at the end of the hall. As he fed change into the machine, he again noticed the blond he had seen in the parking lot. She was coming down the hallway from the opposite direction, carrying her flowers. She stopped outside of Bull's room and glanced briefly in Ward's direction. He pretended he hadn't noticed her and got busy selecting his coffee. The woman entered Bull's room, stayed only a few minutes and then left. Ward followed her, but by the time he reached the parking lot, the white Mercedes had pulled away. Something told him the blond was not Bull's relative.

Back in Bull's room, Ward searched through the flower basket for a card, but found none. He did find a sticker on the basket. It said: Flowers for Every Occasion, Valley Stream, Long Island. As Ward jotted down the name and address of the flower shop, he looked up in time to catch Bull's sleepy eyes staring at him. A weak smile crossed Bull's face.

Chapter 25: Seawood and Johnny L.

Two days later, Ward headed out to see how Bull was doing. Although Bull's head remained bandaged, and his face was still bruised, he was on the phone. He pointed to a bagel on the tray at the foot of his bed as Ward entered the room. Ward smiled and handed him the bagel.

"Yeah? No kidding. Interesting, really interesting. Okay, man. As soon as I'm up and around I'll come over for a couple of beers. Hang tight!" Bull hung up the phone and took a bite from his bagel. Ward could tell Bull was feeling more like his old self and thanked heaven for the gift of his partner's life.

"Glad to see your appetite is still in fine shape," Ward said.

Bull smiled slightly then touched the side of his face. "Hey, don't make me laugh; it hurts too much."

"Sorry! Now that you're on the mend I wanted to talk to you about something that's been bothering me for a long time."

Bull stopped chewing. "Is this about my mother and father? I heard they gave you a good going over."

"Your parents have a point. They want you to go back to reporting for the newspaper; given what happened to you, I think that might not be a bad idea."

Bull dropped his bagel on his broad chest. "What?" He pried the bagel from his dressing gown.

"I'm saying this for a very selfish reason," Ward added. "I lost Barbara and I nearly lost you. I don't want to see you hurt again. Next time they may finish you off."

Bull's eyes widened. He picked up his bagel and cream cheese and threw it against the wall. It landed cream cheese side against the wall and slowly made its decent to the floor. Both Bull and Ward laughed. "Ouch, I'm not supposed to laugh," Bull said as he gently touched the side of his face. "Hey, I came to you to become a detective. You didn't go out and recruit me. Mom and dad have their lives and I have mine. Before I met you, my life was one sorry-ass, boring assignment after another. What I was doing anyone could do. What kind of a life was that?"

"Yes, but look what happened to you."

"Hey, since becoming your partner, I've had one cool car chase, bugged an office, learned how to tap a few telephone calls and come to love red wine and scotch—and don't forget, I knocked that guy's tooth out. This is what I want to do, and I'll take my chances."

Ward laughed. "Knocking people's teeth out?"

Bull smiled through his bandages. "Yes. Ouch, I'm not supposed to laugh."

"Okay Bull, but at least think about what I've said." Ward paused for a second, his eyebrows furrowing. "You tapped telephone calls? When?"

Bull waved off the question. "Never mind. I was just talking to Ben Getty on the phone when you arrived. He found out who picked up those flowers and delivered them to my room. Get this; it was Susan's mother, Angela. She picked them up herself, and I bet that was Uncle Paul with her in the car. But what doesn't make sense is if they sent two goons after me, why the flowers?"

Ward smiled. "That's an old trademark of the mafia. They send flowers to the family of their victims. Something tells me Angela and Paul did not have you beaten up."

"We know the Dwyer family was not involved in any of the mob's dirty business."

Ward nodded his agreement. "But there was some connection between these families, and I suspect we were getting close to making that connection. What seems clear is everyone wants us to back off this case. Uncle Paul threatened Susan, Tucker tried to buy me off and then when those tactics didn't work and you were on their turf questioning the locals, they came after you."

"Do you think Susan knows any of this?" Bull asked.

"I doubt it, but she has some explaining to do."

Ward dialed Susan's home number and asked if she could meet him at a nearby restaurant. She agreed.

"I'll be back tomorrow. Are you going to be okay?" Ward picked up his coat.

"I'm fine, but could you do me a favor?"

"Of course."

"Could you get me another bagel before you leave?"

###

The Oyster Shell restaurant is one of those 'hole in the wall' restaurants that by all standards of appearance and service belong at the bottom of the heap—the last desperate stop on anyone's journey. One enters it under protest, fully expecting slop in a dish and grunts from an abusive waitress. The soiled menus and limited offerings would make one wonder why the place was busy. But once the food was served, all questions and doubts vanished. Ward was into his second order of oysters when he saw Susan coming up the walk. She spotted him as she passed the window and waved. Ward waved back.

Susan placed her backpack on the seat as she slid into her side of the booth. Ward pointed to the oysters and she wriggled her nose in protest, waving her hand as if she were pushing the plate away. "I never liked them, but thanks anyway."

"I received a letter from your family's lawyer, Mr. John Tucker and met with him. He wants me to drop the case. He says your family is very concerned about your health."

Susan slumped back in her seat and shook her head, her eyes blazing with defiance. "What did he tell you?"

"He said you have a medical condition and your family wants me to leave you alone. They feel your health may be at stake."

"Look, I've had a difficult time with my emotions since I was a child, but what does that have to do with anything? I didn't have this problem till mother decided to take off with some other guy. Trust me, I'll tell you if all this is too much for me, okay?"

"Mr. Tucker...," Ward began.

"Screw Mr. Tucker! If you ask me, he's the slimmest bastard to walk this earth, but, hey, who am I to form an opinion? I'm just poor Susan, the kid who has had nervous breakdowns and is paranoid. Isn't that what Tucker told you?"

Ward nodded.

Susan continued, "You wouldn't want to trust Susan. No! Listen to Tucker, he's really someone to be trusted."

The waiter came over but Ward waved him off.

"Why didn't you tell me you were being treated by a doctor?"

"Isn't it obvious? Would you have agreed to take on this case if you knew I had this condition and these episodes?" Susan tilted her head to one side and stared at him. "Would you?" She didn't give Ward a chance to respond. "No, you would have hung up on me like all the rest."

"All the rest?"

"The other detectives I contacted. I made the mistake of contacting local detectives. They all promised to call me back and meet with me, but they didn't. My boyfriend found out that good Mr. Tucker had put the word out to avoid poor crazy Susan King. That's when we asked Jeff Keller for help and was given your name. Tucker figured I had given up, but I didn't."

Ward decided to fill Susan in on what happened to Bull.

"God, Ward, I'm so sorry. You have no idea who did this?"

"You know the Gerberti family?"

"Sure, everyone in Seawood knows them. They were part of the local mafia. I went to school with some of their kids, but we never knew for sure. Our parents never talked about that family. It was just rumors to most of us. And we were too scared to ask."

"Did your grandmother or anyone in your family ever mention being involved with the Gerberti business?"

"What? My family involved with them? In what way?"

"You didn't answer my question. Did anyone ever mention the Gerberti and any dealings your family might have had with them?"

Susan thought hard for a moment then shook her head. "No never. Did you find something to link them to my family?"

"Not directly, but there is the possibility the Gerbertis were involved in some way with your family's boating business."

"Impossible! My grandmother was religious and my uncles honest. They would never be involved in anything illegal. When they were young they probably played with their kids when they moved to the neighborhood, but Elizabeth never spoke of any Gerberti members in regards to our family fishing business. I know Uncle Paul was good friends with Rafael Gerberti when they were teenagers."

"You told me Elizabeth was very upset about something in her past, something she kept as a secret but needed to get off her chest. If your family was somehow connected to the Gerberti family; that might have been the dark secret weighing heavily on her mind."

Gallery of the Chosen

Susan took a deep breath. "I don't know. I need some time to think about what you've said, but Elizabeth would never get involved with crime. However, I can tell you Elizabeth did write about Johnny Lynks in her diaries." Susan reached into her bag and pulled out three small, leather bound books. Bookmarks stuck out from each book. She opened the first diary dated 1926-37. "Here's Elizabeth's first mention of Lynks." Susan pushed the book across the table. The date was September 1936. The passage read: *God help us, my greatest fear has come true. JL is in Seawood. He has been hanging around the docks and the boat.*

"Then two weeks later she wrote this," *JL is working in town. I saw him down by the piers and walked past him without a word. He is a constant threat. I can tell the boys are worried, but they say nothing. We keep our silence. I pray no one finds out.*

"There is nothing for months. But then when Uncle Pete died, grandmother wrote the following, *Pete was pulled from the sea today. My poor brother, God grant him peace. JL was at his funeral. I saw him talking to Todd. I pray he doesn't find out.*

"When her husband, Todd, died, Elizabeth wrote this, *JL called to offer his condolences. I hate him.*

"Finally, there is a reference to something going on in town that I can't make sense of, but the initials JL are mentioned." Ward read the entry:

It has started. Poor girl. No one is saying why she did it. Paul and Al are all over the place. Paul's friend, Rafael is beside himself with rage. I heard them mention JL and someone named Bertini. They were talking about finding this Bertini. I heard Paul talking on the phone to Rafael. Paul said maybe this is the only way.

Ward leaned back and reread the passages. It was clear Elizabeth knew Lynks before he arrived in Seawood and that she feared him. She must have known him when the family lived in New York. When Lynks showed up at Seawood, he would have been in his twenties and Elizabeth around twenty-three. For some reason, the Dwyers feared Lynks. Why was he such a threat? The statement about the girl made no sense, except that Bertini was at the center of their anger. Elizabeth didn't seem to know of the relationship between Lynks and Bertini. Ward looked at Susan. "Did your grandmother keep diaries when she lived in New York?"

"I don't think so. The first diary is dated 1926, the year the family moved from New York City to Seawood." Susan leaned forward. "Ward, who was this Johnny Lynks? I know you know something. How is he connected to Elizabeth?"

"He was somehow involved with your family and maybe the Gerbertis, but right now I am as much in the dark as you are. Susan, what does your mother look like?"

"My Mother?" Susan gave Ward a suspicious look. "Why?"

"Well, a woman came into the hospital with some flowers for Bull. I think it might have been your mother."

"Can you describe her?"

"She was tall, blond and dressed professionally. I'd say she was somewhere in her early fifties. She was driving a white Mercedes, an older model."

"That's Angela all right, but why would my mother take flowers to Bull? She doesn't even know him."

"I intend to find the answer to that question."

"Well, you'll have an opportunity to ask her in person." Susan reached in her bag, pulled out an envelope and handed it to Ward. "My mother asked that I give this to you."

Ward opened the envelope, read its contents and looked up at Susan. "Your mother and Paul want to meet me. She gives me directions on when and where." Ward reread the letter. "They say they will answer all my questions at the meeting and share something about the family's past that will explain why Elizabeth made her request. That's weird. They've been trying to get rid of me, so what could have motivated them to ask for a face-to-face? After what happened to Bull, I can't imagine them thinking I would fall for a setup like this. But the fact that Angela wrote and signed this letter suggests this is a different kind of meeting. Do you have any idea what might have motivated them to call this meeting and tell me about their past?"

Susan smiled and nodded. "Elizabeth's diaries. Angela asked where the diaries went and when I told her I had them and you had asked me to look for information on Johnny Lynks, she nearly fainted. I heard her talking to Paul and someone else on the phone later that night. They were having a heated discussion, especially when she talked with Paul. Next day, she handed me this letter.

"She said they would explain everything at the meeting. She also told me that I was not invited. But I don't care; I think we are getting closer to knowing why Elizabeth made that strange request. Sorry, but I have to go."

Susan slid out of the booth and picked up her bag. "Oh, she told me to tell you that Rafael Gerberti would also be at the meeting."

Peter Saunders

Chapter 26: The Rendezvous

Bull's recovery had gone well and it was not long before he was back in New Rochelle continuing his detective work. A week before meeting with Angela, Paul Dwyer and Rafael Gerberti, Ward and Bull visited Lieutenant Keller and his officers in Manhattan. Ward briefed everyone on Elizabeth's request and the possible discovery of the Lynks body. Bull filled them in on the Dwyer background, explaining their claim to docking space at Seawood and the strange behavior of both the Gerberti and Agrelo families.

When they finished, Keller warned that the meeting with the Dwyers could be another trap, like the one Bull fell into. "My department will provide as much protection as possible, but you are still taking an enormous risk," he said.

Bull asked to go with his partner as backup but Keller said that would just complicate things. Keller turned and faced Ward. "Even though Rafael has no criminal record, the family will not leave him unprotected. He knows too much. His meeting with you is extraordinary considering he's been such an elusive character all his life. I'll bet most of our officers who have dealt with the Gerberti family over the years have no idea what he even looks like. Still, I suspect their goons will surround him and be armed. They will not leave the two of you alone."

Ward nodded. "I understand, but the fact that Rafael wants to be at this meeting confirms the fact that there's some connection between the families. What puzzles me is why they would even discuss this with me. Even with Elizabeth's diary entries, there really is little evidence to pin anything on the Dwyers or anyone else for that matter. And the Gerberti are too powerful to let any of this stick in a court of law."

Keller shook his head. "I just don't like it. What do you hope to gain? I know you believe the Gerberti family may have been involved with your wife's murder despite all evidence to the contrary, but do you really believe they would admit this to you?"

"No, but if you're right and they were not involved, they may know who did it."

Keller leaned back and tossed his pencil on the table in frustration. "Sure, but remember these families watch each other's backs. I doubt you'll find what you're looking for, but go ahead and try. We've been after the Gerberti family for years. Maybe you will come back with something we can use. As I said, we'll provide as much protection as we can. There's a chance they're using Rafael and the Dwyer family to get to you. If you were meeting with just the Dwyer clan, we wouldn't be having this conversation, but with a Gerberti in the mix, the risks and stakes are very high on all sides." Keller smiled. "Everyone knows you've been a major pain for them over the years. I just hope your involvement in this case isn't the straw that breaks the camel's back."

Ward returned his smile. "That makes two of us."

Ward glanced briefly in the rearview mirror as he drove through New Rochelle in the early morning on the day of their meeting. Michelle was asleep in the back seat, while Bull sat in the passenger seat wearing his headset, absorbed in music. Ward's passengers were there for good luck. They insisted on going and would wait at the pickup site till Ward returned.

"Don't argue, I am coming," Michelle insisted.

"Ditto for me," Bull added.

By the time they reached the Throgs Neck Bridge, the rising sun had bathed the bay below and the island beyond in a golden glow. It was at that moment when everything seemed possible, when all that is dark and wrong loses its hold on the world and sinks beneath the ocean's glistening surface. Life seemed to have taken its own course, rising up and out in directions no one could predict. Ward's wife and Susan's grandmother were separated by generations and had never met, but now, by one of life's strange twists, their lives had been brought together. The big question was why had the families agreed to meet after trying so hard to get Ward to drop the case? And why did Susan's mother request he meet with Paul and Rafael? Ward was sure Johnny Lynks was somehow at the heart of all his questions.

Gallery of the Chosen

Nothing seemed to make much sense unless, as Jeff Keller suggested, Ward was walking into a trap. The terms of the meeting were very clear: No cops, no guns, just Ward. He was to meet them at the Oak Beach pier and that's all he knew.

Murdering him seemed highly unlikely. The Gerbertis weren't fools. They knew the police would be nearby with helicopters only minutes away. Keller had arranged for the New York Patrol Bureau to be available with the Coast Guard as backup. Still, too much was unknown.

As they neared Point Lookout, Ward could see Keller waving to them from the police boat moored at the pier. "We're here," Ward announced as Michelle stirred and Bull removed his headset. Ward pulled into the lot, parked, and the three friends followed the walkway out to the cruiser.

"Good morning, sleepy heads," Keller said as they climbed on board and were led below where three officers stood bent over a small table examining a map.

Jeff made the introductions. "Say hello to Captain Bruce Bronzer of the NYPD and his assistants, officers Monica Wodge and Miguel Castandes of the Coast Guard. We'll be their guests. Captain Bronzer will be in charge of this operation so I will ask him to fill you in on the details."

Captain Bronzer looked up and gave the three newcomers the once over. From the way he chewed on his unlit cigar, it was clear he meant business. Officer Wodge, who looked like she was right out of the Academy, gave a brief nod, while Castandes merely stood back and gave the floor to Bronzer.

Bronzer removed the cigar stub from his mouth and put it in his shirt pocket. "No, guests," he declared as he eyed Michelle and Bull.

Keller gave Ward his don't mess with the man look.

Ward put his hand on Bull's shoulder. "Mr. Toolman and Ms. LaGrange are my associates. They…"

"I don't care who they are. They're not invited to this party. Officer Wodge will escort them upstairs."

Ward was about to argue when Michelle gently touched his arm and, pulling Bull after her, they made their way back to the deck. Captain Bronzer took a seat while Ward and Keller took seats on the opposite side of the table. Bronzer turned the map to them to look at and pointed to a spot.

"My understanding is that you are to be picked up at eight hundred hours here at Oak Beach. You are to be alone and unarmed. Is that correct?"

Ward nodded.

Bronzer moved his chubby finger along the map. "We have been surveying this area for the past week. Several of the Gerbertis' powerboats have been active, and, early this morning one of their yachts arrived. It's pretty clear your meeting will take place on the yacht. We have kept our patrol boats out of sight, and as soon as I'm finished here, we'll move them to the Lower Bay area. You will remain on the pier till the Gerbertis pick you up. Keller will station his car just behind the dunes and a patrol boat will be nearby. We've agreed not to intervene under one condition."

"And that would be?" Ward asked.

"That you wear a bug."

"They'll search me."

Bronzer smirked and glanced briefly at the junior officers to make sure they were listening. "That's what we expect they'll do." He reached into his leather briefcase. "This is what they will be looking for." He lifted out a standard, small audio transmitter that strapped to the chest. "But you will not be wearing this." Bronzer put it back in his case and pulled out a watch.

"A watch?" Ward asked.

Bronzer held the watch up. "Looks like a watch, doesn't it? But it's a micro recorder. Just press the crystal down once and it begins taping all that's said. Press it twice and it sends a distress signal to our patrol boat."

Bronzer put the watch on the table. "We tested this little baby yesterday all along the shore and as long as we stay within a two-mile radius, our receivers will pick up the distress signal. It's important that you activate the recorder and if necessary, the signal, because that's the only way we'll know you're in trouble. And if you and the watch should end up at the bottom of the Sound, as long as you activate the distress signal, we'll know where to find the watch and what's left of you."

Keller looked uneasy. "How do we know they don't know about this device?"

Bronzer answered without hesitating. "Well, they might. You see it was developed at MIT last year and sent out for independent testing. If there was a leak, then what they would have heard is that our reports claimed that this device was not reliable so we dumped it. I think we're okay." Bronzer stared at Ward. "You know the reputation of the Gerberti, so I don't have to tell you that going out there is risky."

Ward nodded. "That's what I have agreed to."

"That's fine with me, but I know these creeps. They don't take prisoners."

Ward interrupted Bronzer mid-sentence. "I'll wear the watch."

It was clear Bronzer didn't like being interrupted. Officer Castandes gave Ward a brief glance and slowly inched away. Bronzer removed the cigar from his pocket and shoved it back in his mouth. "I've spent half my career hunting down Gerberti scum. I have a damn good track record. And do you know how I earned that record?"

"I have a feeling you're going to tell me," Ward said.

"You bet I'm going to tell you. They hate my guts, but they respect me because I'm as ruthless as they are. Officially, I'm here to protect you and see that justice is done. Off the record, I don't give a damn what happens to you. If you're stupid enough to go out there alone, that's your business. You won't be armed, but their boys will definitely be armed. We have an opportunity here to nail one, maybe more of the Gerbertis. What we need is a name, anything that would link them to any of our ongoing investigations—something that would let us put one of them away. If they confess to Lynks' murder that will be enough for us to bring Rafael and his friend Paul in for questioning. The families will not be happy and may be willing to bargain for their release. That would be ideal for us. This is a rare opportunity so don't fuck things up, Emerson. Do we understand each other?" He leaned toward Ward and cupped his ear, waiting for a response.

Keller nudged Ward under the table. Ward took a deep breath and forced a half smile. "Yes, I understand."

Bronzer eyed Ward silently for a minute or two. "Good. Your job is to get them to talk. My job will be to nail them once we get the goods on tape."

Keller tried to move the conversation along. "So, assuming we get some names and something that could be used in court on tape, what's next?"

Bronzer pointed to a channel on the map and looked at Ward. "You are to agree to whatever deal they want and then ask to be dropped off inside Rockaway Peninsula. Once you are off their cruiser and we have the watch, we'll cut off their exit. They'll then try to escape through the inner channel, but officers Wodge and Castandes will proceed to close the net. We have no idea how many men may be on board, but we do know that there are three Donzis cruisers stationed nearby and they are all registered with the Gerberti family. We have undercover personnel on the pier and some in smaller boats all along the inlet. They will be in constant communication with me. As soon as you hit the pier, give the watch to the officer who will be waiting for you and then get the hell out of there. We'll take care of the rest."

From the look on Bronzer's face, Ward could tell he was very pleased with the way he had planned the whole thing. Bronzer clearly had visions of a promotion and front-page coverage in all the papers. Ward didn't mind that, but he hated the way the Bronzers of the world pushed their way around. Ward slipped on the watch as Bronzer stood up. "Time to go."

As they reached the upper deck, Ward shook Bull's hand. "Take care of everything till I get back." There was a brief awkward silence between them as they made eye contact.

Bull turned and headed for Keller's car.

Michelle took Ward's hand and followed Bull to the car. Ward kissed her, holding her close. Bull lowered the backseat window. "Michelle, we have to go."

She stood back and looked into Ward's eyes. "Now, you be careful, you understand? No trying to be a hero."

Ward smiled. "I promise. I'll be back by noon. I love you, Michelle," he whispered. With that, Michelle joined Bull in Keller's car and they drove away. Ward remembered how casually he had left his wife on the day she was murdered. How he had wanted that moment back so he could tell Barbara he loved her. This time things were different.

Chapter 27: The Meeting

Ward stood on the Oak Beach pier watching Jeff Keller's car slowly retreat down the unpaved road toward the parkway. The police patrol boat had already pulled away and headed for the Lower New York Bay. Offshore, in the middle of the inlet, a 45-foot Donzi ZX powerboat waited. Ward stood alone on the pier. As soon as Keller's car disappeared and the patrol cruiser was out of sight, one of the Donzi roared to life and raced toward Ward. Angela King, who was seated next to the captain, stood up as the large boat pulled alongside the pier. She motioned Ward to join her as she moved to the back seat. In minutes, the boat was speeding out of the inlet, headed for the large yacht and the two identical Donzis guarding the yacht, just beyond Fire Island.

Men with binoculars stood on the yacht and the Donzis, scanning the horizon to make sure the police boats kept their distance. When the Donzi carrying Angela and Ward arrived at the yacht, two men wearing shoulder holsters moored the boats together. No one spoke. Angela climbed up the ladder and stepped onto the deck. Ward followed. One of the bodyguards approached Ward, frisked him thoroughly, pulling photocopied pages from Ward's shirt pocket. He quickly unfolded the pages and handed them to his partner who glanced at their contents. The pages were then returned to Ward who put them back in his pocket. They ignored the watch on Ward's wrist.

Angela led Ward to a side door that opened to the spacious lower deck. Inside stood two more bodyguards who eyed Ward closely. One of them frisked Ward a second time and then allowed him to proceed. His partner then led them to the bow of the boat and took up a position across from a rectangular table where two elderly men sat next to each other. One of the white-haired men stood with some difficulty and then spoke.

"I'm Paul Dwyer. This is my good friend Rafael Gerberti. Have a seat." Dwyer might have been at least six feet four inches if he hadn't been slightly stooped over. His clothes were badly wrinkled and stained, and his sweater bore small holes. He had a full head of hair that needed cutting. His bushy, arched eyebrows suggested perpetual anger. His face, a sickly yellow, was drawn. His voice carried a nervous edge and his hand shook as he pointed to the seat opposite his. Ward sat down, waiting patiently as Angela went around the table and sat next to her uncle. Ward fingered his watch but didn't activate it.

Rafael Gerberti sat next to Paul Dwyer. He was impeccably dressed. Rafael had the thickest pair of eyeglasses Ward had ever seen. Fish eyes. He has fish eyes, Ward thought. The description given by Bertini's male nurse at the veteran's nursing home popped into Ward's head. This had to be the mysterious Mr. R. who continued paying Bertini's medical expenses.

Paul Dwyer lowered himself into his seat and began. "What do you want? Money?"

Ward didn't hesitate. "No, no money. I want to know who killed Johnny Lynks and who killed my wife."

Dwyer responded with a puzzled expression on his face. "I don't know what you're talking about." Rafael Gerberti merely stared at Ward. Dwyer continued, "Don't bullshit us. Tell us how much you want."

Ward shook his head. "I told you, I don't want your money. I want to know who killed . . . "

Dwyer cut him off. "The hell you don't. I know your type, bottom feeders preying on whatever comes your way, living off of the weak. My niece was easy pickings, wasn't she? She was still in shock from the loss of her grandmother and that made your job a hell of a lot easier, didn't it? And your young friend, what's his name? Toolman? You used him the same way you used my niece." Dwyer's hands shook uncontrollably now. "You bastard. I should have killed you myself."

Angela took her uncle's shaking hands in hers. "Paul, don't." Dwyer struggled to stand, nearly knocking his chair over. Ward stood to help, but one of the bodyguards shoved him back into his chair. Angela waved the bodyguard off as she steadied her uncle.

Dwyer stared at her, pleading. "I can't take this anymore. He'll destroy our family if we don't stop him."

Angela squeezed his hands gently. "Paul, we won't let that happen." Taking him by the arm, Angela led him toward the stern.

Rafael Gerberti had not taken his eyes off of Ward. He studied him closely throughout the entire exchange. Finally he broke his silence, drawing Ward's attention back to the table. "What do you know about Johnny Lynks?"

"I know he came across something he was not supposed to, something that both the Dwyers and your family could not let come to light. My guess is that Lynks found out about your family's gambling businesses up and down the Sound. Maybe he wanted a cut. I know someone knocked Lynks off and buried him in the Dwyer family plot. Elizabeth knew Lynks was down there. In her final days, her conscience got to her, so she pleaded to be buried somewhere else. For all I know, maybe she killed Lynks. I don't know who actually did it, but from the entries in her diary, it won't take the police long to figure out who killed him. You may want to read what Elizabeth had to say about Lynks and her family and yours." Ward pulled out the photocopied sheets from his pocket and tossed them across the table.

Rafael carefully unfolded the pages and read the contents, then handed them back to Ward. He took a handkerchief from inside his coat pocket, removed his thick glasses and began cleaning the lenses as he spoke almost in a whisper. "Your wife was murdered?"

Ward's body stiffened. "Yes."

"I'm very sorry to hear that, but why would we know who murdered her?"

Ward leaned slightly forward, his finger activating the watch's recorder. A bodyguard moved toward Ward, his hand on his gun but Rafael waved him off. Ward responded, "Why? Because I was close to breaking up a drug syndicate at the time - a syndicate your family had an interest in. There were signs I was getting close to breaking the case when someone murdered my wife. Does all this help refresh your memory?"

Rafael shook his head. "I cannot speak for the other members of my family, but I have no idea who killed your wife. Regarding Johnny Lynks, that is another story. Mr. Emerson, are you capable of feeling compassion?" The puzzled expression on Ward's face prompted Gerberti to add, "Can you show compassion for a man more sinned against than sinning?" He touched the center of his chest. "Have you ever felt, deep within you, a sympathy for those innocents who suffer at the hands of others? From what I've heard about you, I suspect you have felt such feelings. Indeed, perhaps your career is a testimony to your compassion for others. Am I right?"

Something seemed unmistakably decent about Rafael from the words he spoke and the gentle way they were spoken. "Yes, I believe in compassion. I have felt those feelings,"

Rafael seemed relieved. "I am glad, because if we cannot feel compassion for others, then we, as a race, are doomed. Would you not agree?"

Ward nodded but smiled.

Rafael looked surprised by Ward's reaction. "You find my question funny?"

"No. I'm smiling because somehow I find it difficult making a connection between compassion and your family's long history of extortion, murder and God knows what else."

Rafael pressed on. "You didn't answer my question. Isn't it compassion that makes us human and redeems us? Don't you agree?"

Ward thought for a moment. "Well, I've never thought of it that way, but yes, I would agree."

"Good, I am glad we have this in common. You have asked for the truth. And I am prepared to give you the truth about Johnny Lynks in return for your compassion. That is all I ask."

Gerberti spoke to the bodyguard. "Ask Paul and Angela if they would rejoin us."

When they had returned, Rafael began, "I've made a pact with Mr. Emerson. I told him we will tell him the truth about Johnny Lynks in return for his compassion." Rafael caught the attention of his bodyguard. "Go join the others and wait till I call you." The bodyguard began to protest, but Rafael reassured him. "It's okay. He's unarmed. Go wait with the others."

Dwyer sat with his head bowed and said nothing.

"Paul, we must trust him. We must give him a chance to prove himself. Tell him why Lynks was murdered."

Paul Dwyer continued sitting with his head lowered. The boat rocked gently as the four sat in silence waiting. Finally, Dwyer looked up and began.

Peter Saunders

Chapter 28: Lost Childhood

July had been incredibly hot that summer of nineteen hundred twenty-four. It broke all records in New York City. It was stuffy and unbearably hot in the dark little room the five Dwyer children shared on the eighth floor of the eastside tenements. There was no breeze, no movement of the curtains, no relief or escape from the oppressive heat. The only sounds were the soft voices of a few weary souls who retreated to the building's front stoop, unable to sleep.

The children's room was at the end of a long, narrow hallway leading to two other bedrooms, a bathroom, a kitchen, a small living room and the front door of the apartment. The family's twenty-four year old renter, Johnny Lynks, occupied the room closest to the children's room.

In the children's room, the older boys, twins Edward and Albert, age eleven, slept in bunk beds against one wall. Their brother, Peter, age nine, shared the bottom bunk with Albert. Paul, age seven, was in a cot pushed up against the bunk bed. Across from the boys' beds, against the other wall, was Elizabeth's bed. She was thirteen and responsible for putting the boys to sleep. Little Paul and Peter had gone to sleep immediately after she read their favorite story about a brave little rat that lived on an island in the great North Country.

Edward and Albert had a harder time getting to sleep. Elizabeth promised that if they closed their eyes and went to sleep, she would take them to the candy store the next day and buy them gum. Around eleven p.m., they drifted off. The door to their room was open in the hope that whatever breeze there might be would make its way into the room.

The renter was not in his room. He stood in the shadow-filled hallway, patiently waiting for silence to settle over the apartment.

That night Elizabeth dreamed her last childhood dream. In sleep, she saw a glistening lake with its wide-open expanse of blue water. She and the children sat on a raft, skippered by the brave little rat they had read about in the storybook. They grew excited at the great adventures about to begin.

The raft's sail billowed out, pulling them toward mysterious islands ahead, islands floating on the horizon like tiny jewels. And then the raft, the islands and the dream faded forever.

There was no warning, just a faint awareness of covers being pulled back and the weight of a large body settling next to her. Elizabeth felt a hand over her mouth and when she opened her eyes the renter, Johnny Lynks, was beside her, whispering, telling her to stay quiet and still. Elizabeth didn't understand what was happening. Johnny had been their friend, taking them to the park, playing games, telling them jokes and stories. She stared at him, confused and frightened. He whispered warnings to her. If she wasn't quiet, she would wake her brothers and her parents, and it would be her fault. He told her this was a new game that would not hurt; then his hand lifted her nightgown and forced her legs apart.

On the sweltering streets below there was no breeze, just the suffocating heat and the occasional rattle of the elevated subway.

Over the months that followed, Lynks' visits continued. And each time he added a new threat, warning that he would harm her brothers or her mother if she told, and the harm that came to them would be her fault. Once, in desperation, Elizabeth begged her mother to get rid of Lynks. "We need his rent money," her mother said. "And he's a wonderful help with the boys." Elizabeth pleaded, "I'll get a job so we won't need a renter." Her mother just laughed.

One summer weekend, Elizabeth stayed over at a friend's house. When she returned home Sunday evening, she discovered Lynks had borrowed a car and taken the boys to an amusement park in Jersey. On the way home, he stopped at an abandoned farm, saying they could play in the old barn. First he cornered and raped Albert and then Edward.

At first, nothing was said between Elizabeth and the twins, but she suspected from their erratic behavior what Lynks had done. Months later, Lynks raped Peter and then little Paul. After that, the boys refused to be with Lynks alone. Then when Paul's nightmares began, Johnny Lynks moved out, saying he was taking a new job outside of the city. Not long after Lynks' departure, the children shared their horrible secret. Their mother and father never knew what had happened.

Gallery of the Chosen

When the family finally moved out of the city to Seawood, Long Island, Elizabeth thought that would be the end of Johnny Lynks. The boys' erratic behavior continued getting worse and by the time they were in their early twenties, they had become heavy drinkers and had turned violent.

Elizabeth met and married Todd Dixon. Todd bought a large fishing boat and hired Elizabeth's brothers as his crew. The business thrived. In the summer of 1936, Lynks showed up in town and took a job on the docks. Elizabeth was terrified when her ailing mother told her the news. The secret Elizabeth shared with her brothers would no longer stay buried. She was glad that her mother and father never knew what Lynks had done to the children. Both parents died shortly after Lynks arrived.

One afternoon while shopping at the local market, Elizabeth felt the presence of someone staring at her. It was Lynks. He approached and took a firm hold of her arm. He warned that he would kill one of her brothers if she told anyone about his past. Then he left.

The boys went crazy. "We should kill Lynks," Peter said, but Albert and Edward managed to calm their brother. They decided to wait and see what Lynks' plans were.

For a while he left everyone alone and became popular in town, but the boys kept an eye on him. They knew better.

One morning, Peter took the small motorboat and went fishing at sunrise as he always did on his day off. Just outside the jetty, Lynks was waiting for him. A non-swimmer, Peter didn't stand a chanced once Lynks knocked him out of the boat. No one suspected Lynks and when alcohol was found in Peter's blood, the local police assumed he was drunk and had fallen overboard. What no one knew was that Peter had asked to meet Lynks on that morning. Later Paul found his brother's handgun missing and knew the truth. Their brother had gone to kill Lynks but had failed. The gun was never found.

Later that year Todd died from a heart attack after a mysterious fire broke out on the fishing boat. Elizabeth was pregnant with Angela, so Angela never knew her father. The family suspected Lynks had something to do with the fire, but couldn't prove it. Not long after that Edward was found dead, a suicide note by his side. Albert's drinking increased and he began to have serious health problems.

"I kept telling them that we should kill Lynks before he killed us all." Paul Dwyer's voice broke as he told the story, and he began sobbing. Waving his hand, he indicated he could no longer continue.

Rafael, who had sat quietly through Paul's confession, spoke. "That's okay, Paul. I'll finish." He looked directly at Ward. "Paul is family to me. When he moved into Seawood, we became the best of friends and shared everything, but he did not tell me about Lynks. He should have told me what Lynks had done to him and his family, but he didn't. I have learned to forgive him for that, for had I known, we might have saved my cousin Maria Agrelo. You see Lynks had not changed."

Rafael continued, "He had learned to pick his victims carefully and somehow he found Maria. The family didn't know this, but he would meet her after school and walk her part of the way home. She was only sixteen and strong-willed. The Gerberti and Agrelo families are Catholic and are very protective. At this time, our families were not in competition, and they looked after each other.

"We didn't know Maria agreed to meet Lynks after school one afternoon down by the old storage houses. Lynks had brought someone along to keep watch. He'd chosen a poor, simple soul named Bertini, who told me later that Lynks said he was going to propose to my cousin."

There was a long pause as Rafael collected himself for what he had to say next. "Lynks didn't propose. He raped Maria just as he had raped all the others. And later, when Maria discovered she was pregnant, Bertini told me she begged Lynks to marry her, but he merely laughed. Two days later she slit her wrists.

"Our families tried to hide the truth from the community, but Seawood is a small village. The autopsy revealed that Maria was pregnant, but we didn't know who was responsible. Lynks had threatened Bertini, saying he would kill him if he stayed in Seawood, so Bertini fled, and, of course, everyone suspected he had done it. My family put a contract out on Bertini. Meanwhile, Lynks behaved himself.

"Then one day, I got a call from a friend out at the track. He told me a guy who looked like Bertini but who was going under a different name had said something about my cousin, Maria. So Paul, Tony Agrelo and I grabbed Bertini and got the truth out of him."

Gallery of the Chosen

Rafael paused and sat staring into nothingness, reliving the horrible past. "Once we knew about Lynks, the rest was easy. Paul contacted Lynks and told him Elizabeth missed him and wanted to see him. They were to meet on the old dirt road by the marsh fields, about a mile from the cemetery. Lynks arrived around eleven and got into Elizabeth's car. We grabbed the bastard and drove to the cemetery. We had dug a grave at Elizabeth's family plot and had a box waiting for Lynks. We tied him up, castrated him and threw him into the box. We buried him alive. Paul promised he would dig Lynks up and move him later, but word that Lynks was missing caused quite a stir. The police checked his apartment and found all his clothes and possessions, so they were certain he didn't leave town. When the local newspapers asked the people of Seawood to contact the police if they had any information about his whereabouts, Paul couldn't risk moving Lynks' body."

Rafael looked at his friend Paul. Angela had her arms around him and was whispering softly to comfort him. "This meeting is over, Mr. Emerson. I pray you consider the trauma our families have experienced." Rafael signaled for the bodyguard to join them. "Tony, take Mr. Emerson back to the dock."

###

The Donzi pulled slowly away from the yacht and headed toward the Rockaway Peninsula. Ward stared at the micro recording watch on his wrist. Rafael's words repeated in his head: "Can you show compassion for a man more sinned against than sinning?" When the Donzi reached the halfway point, Ward removed the watch from his wrist and tossed it into the sea. A police helicopter followed at a safe distance. From the cockpit, the pilot thought he saw a brief flash of reflected light that quickly disappeared as the watch sank beneath the ocean's surface.

Peter Saunders

Chapter 29: The Lead

"So how did Bronzer take your disappearing act?" Bull asked, a smile stretching across his face from ear to ear. They were seated at the Thruway diner.

Ward grinned back. "Well, let's just say Keller had to work overtime on the guy's bruised ego. I called and told him there was no confession from either Rafael Gerberti or Paul Dwyer, so there was nothing we could pin on anyone. And I told him I had no idea how the watch slipped off my wrist. Unfortunately, because the distress signal was not activated, they will not be able to find it."

Janet delivered their orders and winked at Bull, who blushed deeply. She looked at Ward as she tore the bill from her order pad and placed it on the table. "When is your partner going to pop the question to some lucky lady?"

Ward caught the twinkle in Janet's eye and went along for the ride. "Bull? Don't rush the guy. His hands are full fighting off the ladies."

Bull faked a hearty laugh "Very funny, very funny."

Janet whispered in Bull's ear, "Seriously Vincent, if you run out of prospects I have a friend who is looking for a hunk of a man to cook for. She's just your type." Janet gave Bull a kiss on the cheek and left.

Bull wiped his cheek with the back of his hand, checking to see if any lipstick had stuck to his face.

Ward smiled and continued. "You asked me about Bronzer, right? Keller says he'll calm down, eventually."

Bull swallowed hard. "So you expect me to believe that the watch just slipped off your wrist?" He held up his right arm, pulled his sleeve up exposing his own watchband wrapped securely around his wrist and gave his watch a hard tug. The watch didn't budge. Bull raised his eyebrows and nodded in the direction of the watch.

Ward shrugged his shoulders in defense. "Hey, what can I say? I was just as surprised as you that the thing went missing."

Bull pulled his sleeve back down. "Well, what I hear is the helicopter pilot thought he saw you toss something overboard."

Ward gave Bull his best impression of a falsely accused man. "Not possible. It must have been the glare from the boat's windshield he saw. Besides, who are you going to believe—your partner or some pilot who thought he saw something bright fall into the sea?"

Bull shifted gears. "Never mind that. Are you going to tell me what you, old man Dwyer and Rafael Gerberti discussed?"

Ward was about to answer when Janet returned. "Vincent, there's a call for you upfront."

Bull went to the front desk and took the call. "Hey, what's up? Where? When?" He pulled a pen from his pocket and began writing. "Got it. I owe you big time, Sid." He signaled to Janet that he wanted his slices of pie boxed.

"So who was that?" Ward asked as Bull sat down.

"Sid Feldman, the owner of the best men's store in White Plains. He says a guy who looked like Timothy Stoddard came into his store and bought some expensive clothes."

Ward looked surprised. "You mean Katherine Barkley's lover boy, the guy they've been looking for in the Barkley art heist?"

Bull nodded. "Yup, that's the guy."

Ward gave Bull a quizzical look. "What makes Sid think it's Stoddard?"

Bull opened his wallet and pulled out the picture of Katherine Barkley at NYU. "I showed him this picture. I remembered what Katherine said about Stoddard being very fussy about his clothes so I figured since there are only a few places between here and Tarrytown that carry the good labels, if he was still somewhere in this part of Westchester, he would visit Sid's store. I made a copy of the photo and gave it to Sid. Stoddard showed up but used a different name and purchased some expensive items that needed alterations. He said he would pick up the clothes, but he did give an address in the Bronx where he was staying." Bull handed Ward the piece of paper with the address. "Looks like he hasn't left the country yet. It might be a dead-end, but it's worth a try."

"Nice work." Ward stood and put money on the table to cover the bill. "I know that area."

"Maybe Stoddard is our killer," Bull suggested as he put on his coat.

Gallery of the Chosen

"I doubt it. As far as we know, Stoddard was involved in only one, possibly two of the heists. And one of the women was murdered in San Francisco when Stoddard was staying with Katharine. Let's pay him a visit. Barkley will be very happy to see him again!" Ward grabbed his coat and headed to the front door.

Bull chased after Ward, passing Janet as she grabbed food boxes off of the shelf.

"Hey, I thought you guys wanted to take your food with you?"

Bull glanced longingly at the food and paused briefly, then decided that Ward would be gone if he waited. "Freeze it."

Thirty minutes later, Ward's car pulled up outside a four-story apartment building standing on a corner next to a vacant lot.

"Did Sid give an apartment number?" Ward asked.

Bull shook his head. "No, but how hard can it be to find our guy in an apartment building this size?"

Ward gave Bull his I know you're being a smart-ass look.

Getting into the building was easy. Someone had propped the front door open with a cinder block. The elevator sat idle on the first floor.

"Let me see that photo again." Ward walked into the foyer and looked at the names of the occupants of the first two apartments on the first floor. He knocked on the first door—the superintendent's apartment. No one answered. Ward moved to the next apartment. After a few knocks, a woman's voice called from behind the door.

"Who is it? What do you want? I don't want anything you're selling."

"Mrs. Kohl, I'm with the police. We need your help identifying someone in this building. I want to show you a photograph."
There was a long pause. "How do I know you're the police and not some robber or salesman? I'm sorry, but you'll have to get someone else to help. Go see Mr. Ross, the superintendent in the next apartment."

"Mr. Ross isn't in. You don't have to come out, Mrs. Kohl. I'll slip a photo under your door and you can tell me if you've seen the man in the photo and know which apartment he lives in. Is that okay?"

There was another long pause. "I guess that's okay."

Ward reached down and slid the photo under her door.

"I've never seen the woman before, but the man is Mr. Diamond in 211. He's helped me with my groceries several times. Has he done something wrong?" The photo reappeared from under the door.

"Thank you for your help. We just want to talk to him."

"He may be away. I haven't seen him for a couple of days."

Ward and Bull headed down the hall to the elevator. Ward propped the elevator door open with a lobby chair so Stoddard couldn't escape using the elevator. Then Ward headed up the stairs nearest the front entrance while Bull ran to the other end of the hallway and started up those stairs.

Coming from opposite directions, they stopped outside apartment 211 and listened. Faint sounds from a television could be heard. Ward pulled his gun from his holster and stood back. Bull backed up, and then charged like a rhino, smashing the doorframe.

Inside the apartment foyer, they found a pool of blood and streaks stretching down the hallway, and then disappearing around a corner. It was clear that a body had been dragged. Moving cautiously, they following the trail of blood. The first doorway they passed led to the kitchen. Bull moved slowly into that room while Ward continued following the trail down the hall and into the living room. Ward paused briefly, calling out Stoddard's name. There was no response.

Ward peeked around the corner, making sure he wouldn't be in the line of fire if Stoddard had a gun. He didn't have to worry. Stretched out on the floor and leaning against the couch was Stoddard's body. His throat had been slashed and his head hung to one side. His chest was covered with blood. Bull joined Ward and together they checked the bathroom and the bedroom. When they were certain no one else was in the apartment, Ward returned to the living room, turned off the television, and dropped heavily into a side chair. He leaned back and stared at the ceiling. The image of Barbara's blood-covered body and her slit throat flashed in his mind.

Bull stared at Stoddard. "God, someone really did a job on this guy. Now we'll never know if he knew who killed your wife and all those other women."

Ward took a deep breath. "Oh, he knew our killer all right. The way Stoddard was murdered suggests his murderer is the man we're looking for. See the way his neck has been sliced open? The guy we're looking for likes to use a large boning knife."

Gallery of the Chosen

Bull's eyes widened as he looked at Stoddard again. "All the women killed looked like this?"

Ward nodded. "Except the murderer positioned the women with their arms crossed, their heads tilted back and locks of their hair placed over their eyes."

Bull began scouring the room, looking for anything that might help. It was clear the rooms had been searched. He went back to the front door and studied the dried pool of blood on the floor, then returned to Stoddard's body and looked at his shoes. "Boss, we have a footprint and it doesn't belong to the victim."

Ward knelt beside Bull as they examined the clear outline of a man's running shoe. "The fact the apartment was searched suggests his murderer came here looking for something significant. My guess is Stoddard wouldn't give it up, so he was murdered."

Bull jumped in. "It looks like Stoddard was planning to leave the country. There's a one-way plane ticket to Paris on the kitchen table. There's also a wallet that's empty except for this card for a local athletic club. He was registered as Bob Johnson."

Ward examined the card. "There's a number written on the back. It's not a telephone number. That's strange."

Bull looked at the card. "What's strange?"

Ward turned the card over. "Well, when we interviewed Katharine, she told us Stoddard was not into sports. Why would he join an athletic club?"

Ward stood up. "Let's check out the athletic club."

###

When Ward and Bull arrived at the athletic club, they discovered a young man around Bull's age at the front desk. Ward pretended to be reading the notices on the bulletin boards. Bull approached the attendant.

"Can I help you?" the man asked.

Bull smiled. "I hope so. My friend Bob Johnson, who is a member, suggested I join this club. I told him I would stop in and check out the facilities. He gave me his card." Bull handed the card to the attendant.

"Oh, he didn't have to give you his card. The number on the back is probably his combination to his locker."

Bull took the card back. "Well, if possible I would like to get a locker near Bob's. We'll be coming together after work."

The attendant smiled. "Absolutely. Let me check to see if we have empty lockers there." The attendant reached for a green binder and flipped quickly through the pages. "Let's see, your friend's locker is on the second floor. You're lucky. Number R11 is vacant and it's right next to Mr. Johnson's locker."

Bull smiled. "That is lucky. Do you mind if I walk around and check out the facilities?"

The attendant put the binder back. "No, not at all."

Bull and Ward headed for the second floor and the R section of lockers. It didn't take long to find Stoddard's locker and open the combination lock. Inside the locker was a leather briefcase, which they removed and took to a small table. They opened the case. Inside was a binder containing detailed lists of paintings and other works of art. There were several contact numbers, but no names. Ward quickly scanned the list of paintings. All of Barkly's paintings were on the list.

Chapter 30: Prisoner in Love

Ward and Bull made copies of the list of paintings and phone numbers found in Stoddard's binder and then turned the binder over to the police. Keller would trace the phone numbers and get back to them. Although Stoddard's material contained no names, Ward had a hunch that the dates referred to actual heists. The list went back six years. A glance at the date listed next to the paintings stolen from Barkley's gallery matched the date the collection disappeared. If Ward was right, Stoddard's murderer was the serial killer and Stoddard was somehow linked to the art heists and the murderer. Ward held his breath as he checked for paintings stolen around the time of Barbara's death. After careful searching he found that two paintings were taken from a well-known gallery in Manhattan two days before her brutal attack. A pattern was emerging; it was pointing to the man he had spent so much time hunting down.

Ward arrived home one evening soon after discovering Stoddard's body to find a message on his answering machine. The unidentified caller suggested Ward pay a visit to Patrick O'Hare at the state federal prison. Professor Rapin had mentioned Patrick O'Hare, saying he knew more about art heists and the illegal sale of stolen paintings than anyone. Privately Ward didn't hold out much hope that such a visit would prove useful. He remembered Rapin's description of O'Hare as talented, crooked, persuasive and charming, but also a major liar.

The federal prison in New Jersey where Patrick O'Hare was doing time had quite a reputation. Officially the prison was known as a low security, federal correctional institution. Unofficially, it was referred to as the resort and its prisoners as celebrities who were pampered, especially those with political and mob connections. Calling it a correctional institution instead of a prison said it all. It was considered the model institution for reforming well-connected offenders and those convicted of white-collar crimes. The weight room, recreational gym, social meeting rooms and classrooms supported the progressive philosophy that all humans have the capacity to change their behavior, if treated humanely.

Even on the outside, except for the chain-linked fence topped with low quality barbed wire, there were few signs this was a prison holding some of the cleverest individuals to grace America's wanted lists.

Ward had called ahead so O'Hare, who was in the fifth year of his seven-year sentence, knew he was coming. Not that O'Hare was going anywhere, of course. Ward did some checking around before his visit and discovered Rapin was not exaggerating when he noted O'Hare's considerable artistic abilities. Directors at three art houses Ward contacted knew O'Hare's name and considered him possibly the best artist in the business at reproducing a painting and passing it off as the original. Two of the directors knew galleries that had purchased his copies thinking they were originals.

The main visitor's room at the prison was large and noisy with dark oak floors, pastel colored walls and comfortable leather furniture. The guard at the door pointed to a distinguished looking man seated at an oak table near a window. As Ward made his way across the room he could feel the inmates sizing him up before they turned back to their card games, chess matches and conversations.

O'Hare was writing a letter. A small table at his side was piled high with glossy art books and poetry collections. O'Hare's silver hair and his strikingly sharp facial features suggested he had descended from a long line of patricians. A file box filled with letters sat next to his writing paper.

O'Hare looked up as Ward approached.

"I'm Ward Emerson."

O'Hare set his pen aside and leaned back. "So, you've come to see how we celebs live." Patrick chuckled to himself. "I'm sorry to report that you've just missed the cocktail hour. However, welcome to our Jersey paradise. To what do I owe the honor?" Before Ward could respond, O'Hare answered his own question. "No, let me guess. There's something you'll be wanting; some information, perhaps?"

Ward feigned a look of amazement. "Hey, what can I say, Patrick? You're a pretty smart guy. You've got my number." Ward eyed the empty chair beside the table. "Yes, I need some information."

O'Hare caught his glance. "Normally I would tell you to get lost, but I'm told this is to be a special visit, and I'm to treat you well. So please have a seat."

Ward sat. "And who would that contact be?"

O'Hare smiled. "Oh, I'll be happy to answer that question if you happen to have a million dollars or a Pissarro or Vermeer hanging in your living room that you'd be willing to part with."

"Sorry, my bank has a limit on withdrawals, and I gave my last Vermeer away a week ago to my favorite charity. But I do have a couple of prints that might brighten your room."

O Hare laughed. "Well, for the life of me, I can't think of a single reason why I should help you. Can you?"

Ward shook his head. "No, but since I'm here I'll ask anyway. I'm looking for a serial killer who murdered my wife and half a dozen other women. I suspect the killer is linked to art heists you may be familiar with. I'm hoping you're paths crossed."

"What was your wife's name?'

"Barbara."

"And you loved your wife?"

"Yes, I loved her very much."

"And your Barbara loved you? She wasn't doing some younger bloke on the side?"

"No, she wasn't like that."

O'Hare laughed. "Are you sure? Don't you know that a fellow can't always tell?"

"I'm sure."

"Then you're a lucky man, a very lucky man, Ward Emerson. I, on the other hand, haven't been so fortunate, until I met my Valerie, that is." O'Hare reached over and picked up a volume of poetry. "Do you like poetry? Did you ever write poetry for your Barbara?" O'Hare turned to a place in the book he had marked with a piece of paper.

"Yes, when we were first dating," Ward responded.

"Did you ever read her the poetry of John Donne?"

"I don't think so."

O'Hare gently rubbed the cover of the volume he was holding. His furrowed eyebrows indicated his disappointment at Ward's response. "Oh, then you've missed a kindred spirit, a wonderful poet and a man who found real love. Unfortunately he was born into the wrong religion and he and his beautiful bride, Anne, were punished their entire lives. And didn't they pay a heavy price for their devotion. Still, society could not break them."

O'Hare closed the volume of poetry. "I'm writing a poem to my Valerie. I'll share a secret. She's my first real love. Can you believe that?" O'Hare chuckled. "A man of my advanced age has found true love for the first time! It's quite remarkable, don't you think? I feel like a pubescent schoolboy."

Ward smiled.

"Now would you like to hear a funny story?" O'Hare set the volume of poetry aside, folded his hands across his chest and settled back in his chair.

"Sure."

"Valerie is not like the women I usually meet in my profession. Don't get me wrong. The other girls were darlings. But the men I work with are rough and crude, like unfinished paintings by untalented novices. All they talk about is how they banged some broad in the morning and another after lunch. Love to them is getting their hands up a skirt and indulging their lower instincts." O'Hare shook his head. "It's really quite pathetic." He glanced briefly at the box of letters by his side and then continued. "As I was saying, for the most part, the men I work with have no eyes to see, and no hearts to feel anything beyond physical pleasure. And I confess, I once shared their weaknesses and deceptions. Then I met Valerie. She has a natural beauty that drew me to her, but there was something in her eyes, in the way she carried herself. It's something precious, like rare art. Well, within a blinking of an eye, wasn't a spark lit and wasn't I an ardent devotee. A woman's beauty and love can unlock something within your soul and like a magnificent painting it shows you a world you didn't know existed. Would you be agreeing with me?"

Ward nodded.

"The tragedy is that most people cannot see or feel real beauty even when it's right in front of them, just as they cannot distinguish a masterpiece by Munch or Renoir from a forgery. All of which is sad, but profitable for me. Anyway, wasn't I about to tell you how I met my Valarie? I was in Wiltshire, England, casing the estate of the Marquis of Bath. My target was Titian's The Flight to Egypt, a truly wonderful piece. Years ago, I would have lifted the painting myself, but now I find it more profitable to my clients and myself if I locate valuable paintings that can easily be stolen. I leave the dirty work to someone else. Well, I could see right away that getting Titian's painting was going to be easy. The security system was antiquated. So I decided to celebrate my good luck. The next day I went to the local pub and there was Valerie. She's a local artist and wasn't she just sitting alone pouring over some books on Hals, a very respectable artist. I had time on my hands, so didn't I strike up a conversation with the young lady." O'Hare suddenly realized that he was rambling along. "Am I boring you?"

"No, not at all. Please continue."

"I'm a professional, so I don't mix work with pleasure. I told her I was a collector, which is only a half lie when you come to think of it." Both Ward and O'Hare laughed. "Our conversations were so natural; it was as if we'd known each other for years. As I said, it was her beauty that drew me to her and her passion that opened my heart. It was like the pull of the moon on the oceans, a natural attraction I couldn't resist. And her insight and knowledge of art was remarkable, but it was her sensitivity to the human heart that inspired me. Hadn't I found my soul mate? I stayed an extra week and forgot completely about Titian's painting. Can you imagine that! I passed up The Flight to Egypt for a strange woman. I had fallen in love with her. Two months after I returned to New York, I turned myself in."

"Really?"

"Cross my heart and may all the saints in heaven judge me on my final day if what I say isn't true." O'Hare looked over at the box of letters. "These are our love letters. Good Lord, I have a crate full of them back in my room; five years' worth of love letters." He paused and then looked up. "So here I sit, a prisoner in love."
O'Hare cleared his throat and tossed his pen into the box of letters.

"I told Valerie the truth about my profession. When they put me in prison, I told her to go find someone else. My colleagues said I should forget her, free her to live her own life; others claim I am wasting my time, for she'll not be waiting for me, no matter what she says. But Valerie just wouldn't let go." O'Hare paused and surveyed the room. "There are men in here whose women have waited fifteen years for them to be free. Think of that! Fifteen years of lost love and lost life. That's true devotion. Still, they are the lucky ones. Many prisoners get letters from their mothers or sisters and that's okay. Having someone waiting for you, who holds you close to his or her heart is a gift that keeps many of us who are in here going. I feel sorry for the others, the ones whose loved one has moved on. I understand it, but I feel sorry for those lost souls. It's a punishment worse than prison." He leaned toward Ward. "Tell me, who do you think murdered your wife?"

O'Hare's question caught Ward off guard. "I don't know for certain. However, like my wife, a number of women were murdered in the vicinity of an art heist. I thought I had the killer when I tracked down a Timothy Stoddard who I know was involved in at least two art heists, but Stoddard was murdered just before I got to him. Whoever murdered Stoddard is probably the serial killer."

"How was she done? How was your Barbara murdered?" O'Hare studied Ward's reaction to his question.

Ward sat silent for a few minutes, and then took a deep breath. "She was abducted and taken to Glen Island Park. Her throat was slashed and her blood smeared across her forehead and down both cheeks. She was not raped or robbed. The murderer cut off some of her hair and placed it over her eyes. Her arms were placed across her chest with her head tilted back exposing her cutthroat. It's as if the murderer were displaying his work. The way she was murdered, matches the profile of women murdered around the time of major art robberies. We have no motive for these murders. The women appear to have been chosen at random. I suspect whoever did this may be someone from a European syndicate sent over to make sure the stolen art makes it safely back after it's lifted; or perhaps it's a hired thief working for one of the families. I'm wondering if you had dealings with anyone who might be capable of such murders."

O'Hare looked down at the letter he was writing and said nothing.

Gallery of the Chosen

"O'Hare, please, give me something. Anything so I can keep going. My wife paid a terrible price; I owe her."

O'Hare looked up and spoke in a soft and measured voice. "I cannot tell you the name of the person I communicated with because he only used his first name, Neils which I suspect is not his own. I can tell you that if the man who murdered your wife and these other women is the man I spoke to then we are talking about an aberration of nature. He's from the Netherlands or somewhere near there. Our paths first crossed in 1956. By that time I was no longer lifting paintings myself, but only making recommendations. The individual I speak of would contact me, take my recommendations and disappear. I would only learn about the heists from the newspapers or, through a transfer of funds to my special account. Often, I had no idea which work of art had been successfully lifted. There are some wonderful families with exquisite taste in art such as the Russ House in Ireland, and Dunmore Castle in Scotland. I know it broke their hearts when some of their treasures went missing. The strange thing is, I sympathized with them. My heart would be broken if some of my treasures were stolen.

"Over a period of years, I suggested an O'Keeffe, Picasso or Rouault be taken. The man I was in contact with asked me what I thought of works by Bouguereau and Waterhouse. I told him I was impressed with their art and felt the critics had unjustly dismissed them in favor of modernist painters. I told him because their paintings were not highly valued on the art market, I did not recommend they be lifted. When we could not get first class works, I suggested he try for something like a Gainsborough. Those are rather boring paintings, but valued nevertheless.

"Around the time a painting I had suggested was lifted in London, I read about the murder of a young woman near the museum where the heist was to take place. The attack occurred a week before the heist. At the time, I did not connect the two events. I had never actually met my mysterious partner, but I did talk to him on the telephone. He was well educated and had a solid grounding in art history and technique. However, he would often rant on about how modernism had suppressed traditional realists, or how private collectors were depriving the public of a higher calling depicted in their paintings.

"He said these paintings were meant to teach, to inspire and to stop the tide of corruption from washing up on our shores. What he meant by corruption washing up on our shores, I have no idea. I was not surprised by his passion, but what was alarming was his use of violent language when he referred to women. A woman's beauty was to inspire art, but to him, women were all whores. It was the role of the artist, he said, to preserve the beauty women represented before the women destroyed it through their imperfections. It was really quite odd. He said women depicted by Bouguereau and the Pre-Raphaelite painters represented the ideal that flesh and blood women should be emulating. It was almost as though the women in their paintings had real lives and depended on their artists to defend them, or some such nonsense. He said natural beauty needs to be captured before decay and corruption begins. The gods demanded it and these artists understood. I made little of the whole thing until it was reported that another woman was murdered around the time a heist I had recommended occurred. It seemed more than just a coincidence that time, so I did a little checking. I discovered that my mysterious contact had threatened two museum directors after they dedicated galleries to modernism and post-modernism. It was clear my contact was delusional or worse, insane."

Ward sat speechless.

O'Hare wrote three names on a piece of paper: Bouguereau, Lord Leighton and Waterhouse. He tapped the paper with his forefinger. "The man I speak of was obsessed with the works of these painters. Follow their trails and no doubt you will find him." O'Hare picked up his pen again. "I am truly sorry for your loss, but I cannot help you beyond what I've told you. I'm not sure the man I speak of is your wife's murderer, but if he is, I hope you find him. Now it's time for you to leave. Good day, Mr. Emerson."

Chapter 31: The Link

Mr. Ryan O'Casey gave Maggie, his border collie, a pat on the head as he snapped the leash onto Maggie's collar and headed for High Park and their evening walk. A seventy-year-old widower, Ryan appreciated the exercise and companionship their daily walks provided.

Although there had only been light snow dustings over the past week, Ryan knew his Toronto suburb would soon receive its fair share of heavy snow blowing in off Lake Ontario. When the snow arrived, he and Maggie would have to shorten their walks and stay nearer the house until spring. Together they headed west along Hewitt Avenue, then north to Indian Road, turning west on Ridout Street and into the park. Once inside, Ryan let Maggie lead the way.

Stiff winds blew directly into Ryan's ruddy face forcing him to turn his back and pause briefly. Cold winds were no problem for Maggie, whose thick coat provided ample protection as she sniffed the ground and tugged on the leash, eager to venture deeper into the Park. They had just passed the Howard Park Tennis Club when the dog stopped abruptly, raised its head, and barked in the direction of the small parking lot behind the clubhouse. Ryan looked at Maggie and then in the direction of the lot, normally vacant at this hour. A van was parked in the shadows at the back of the building.

Ryan pulled on the leash to get his dog's attention, but the dog would not be distracted. "Come on girl, this way. It's only a van." As the wind shifted, Ryan suddenly heard a woman's scream. At that moment, Maggie jerked the leash from Ryan's hand and ran toward the van. "Maggie, come back, come back." Then Ryan heard another scream and rushed after his dog. "Maggie, come back."

When the dog reached the van, she ran to the rear and began barking and pawing furiously at the rear doors. The front passenger door suddenly opened and a woman jumped out, stumbled and ran screaming in Ryan's direction. Reaching him, she fell into his arms, her hands and hair covered with blood. Ryan looked up in time to see the van speed out of the park with his dog in pursuit.

"Maggie, come here!" The dog stopped and headed back to its master as the van raced down the street.

###

Bull stood in Ward's living room, studying his profile in the mirror. The question he was considering was a weighty one: did the expensive, tan leather jacket he bought only two months ago make him look slimmer and sexier? At the time he bought the jacket, he thought the light tan color was perfect for his decidedly masculine physique, but since buying the coat he had learned that the proof was in the seasonal pudding. He had gone about the selection of his clothes all the wrong way. Mabel, who worked at Macy's men's department, had clued Bull in on the mysteries of matching complexions and color shadings to wardrobes. Dieting was important! He could not deny that, but according to Mabel, all the big Hollywood stars knew the secret of matching their clothes to their complexions. She was sure his favorite male stars, Hackman, Redford, McQueen, Pacino, DeNiro and even Eastwood, knew which colors made them look healthier, sexier and more powerful. Bull had bought Mabel lunch when he was shopping at Macy's on Herald Square and in return she gave him a color chart indicating four seasonal color systems and basic skin tone colors. Bull stared at the color chart, his heart beating rapidly. Mabel thought winter was his ideal color season. Bull smiled. Winter, with its cool tones, seemed to enhance his olive-toned skin with its air of European sophistication. But the color tan, the color of his new coat, did not appear in the list of compatible colors. Bull loved the jacket and had paid dearly for it, but he had to confess that now he had doubts. He had given away at least half his wardrobe to charity, convinced that with his new secret weapon, it would be the beginning of a new chapter in his romantic life. But giving away the leather jacket was another matter. Maybe if he dyed his hair that would make the jacket work. His father and mother would kill him and Ward would probably help them.

The sound of a key in the door broke Bull's reverie. He quickly removed his jacket, hung it on the coat rack, and hurried to the couch and sat down.

"Bull?"

"Hey."

Ward hung his coat in the hall closet and joined his partner in the living room.

"What's up?" Bull asked as he put down the magazine he was pretending to be reading.

"Same old, same old," Ward replied as he began sifting through the mail. When he finished, he went to the phone and checked his messages.

Bull stared at his tan jacket and glanced down at the color chart. It was too late to take the jacket back for a refund. He wondered what color hair dye Mabel would suggest.

"Here's a call from my friend in Toronto." Ward pressed the rewind button and listened.

"Ward, it's Jack Timmins. I'm calling because we may have our first real break in your wife's murder case. Looks like the killer might have struck in Toronto, but this time his victim escaped. The woman saw his face and a composite drawing is being made. Call me."

Ward pick up the phone and dialed. "Jack, it's Ward. How the hell are you? I just listened to your message. What makes you think this may be Barbara's killer?"

Jack gave Ward the basic details. "The assailant kept saying something crazy to his victim about the glory of joining the other women as an offering to the gods. He was cutting a piece of her hair off, and then went crazy when he saw her bangs were covering a large birthmark. He started cutting her all over, but she's a fighter and managed to get the knife away from him. She thinks she cut his left cheek pretty badly. The assailant panicked when a dog started pawing at the backdoor of his van. Somehow the woman managed to open the passenger door and jump out. The van drove away, but we have a good idea what the guy looks like."

Ward's heart was racing. "How soon can I interview the woman? We can be there the day after tomorrow. I'll have Jeff Keller call your department to make this official. And Jack, thanks for everything." Ward hung up and went back to his seat. He smiled at Bull. "Have you ever been to Canada?"

Bull nearly jumped off the couch. "Canada? Been to Niagara Falls, but we stayed on the American side. Why?"

"Would you like to join me on a trip to the Great White North?"

Bull smiled back. "You bet your Aunt Tilly I would."

Ward laughed. "Well go home, grab your passport and pack. We're going to Toronto." Ward noticed the tan jacket for the first time. "You might want to wear that leather jacket."

Bull slipped the jacket on and stared at his profile in the mirror. "Boss, do you think this jacket makes me look like a professional detective?"

Ward checked him out. "Absolutely."

Bull smiled. "Canada, watch out; Detective Vincent Toolman is on the case."

Chapter 32: Extending the Net

Officer Jack Timmins was waiting for Ward and Bull at the Toronto Police Station. He led them to the interviewing room where they were introduced to Janet Gibbons, the woman who survived her attacker at High Park. Both Ward and Bull were shocked at Janet's condition. Her face had several wounds across her cheek, neck and lip, all requiring stiches and bandages. Janet was in her twenties, slim, with long dark brown hair, a fair complexion and crystal eyes. Bull wrote something on his notepad and pushed the pad over for Ward to read. *Even with the injuries, she's beautiful. Fits profile of other victims.*

Officer Timmins began. "Miss Gibbons, this is Detective Ward Emerson and his partner Vincent Toolman from New York. They believe the man who attacked you may be someone they have been looking for in regard to the murders of several women. Detective Emerson has some questions for you." Officer Timmins nodded in Ward's direction.

Ward took over. "My partner and I appreciate you granting us this interview. We are very sorry for your injuries and will keep this as short as possible. We realize how difficult it must be reviewing the events of the evening you were attacked."

Janet shook her head. "I'll do whatever I can if it helps you catch that monster. You say he may have murdered several women?"

"Yes."

"How did he kill them?"

"He cut their throats."

Janet stared at Ward and said nothing. After a long pause, she asked, "Were the women sexually assaulted?"

"No. And apparently he also wasn't after their money."

"Why does he kill these woman?"

Ward took a deep breath. "We're not certain, but we believe these are ritualistic killings he performs."

"He was trying to cut off some of my hair when I escaped. What did he want with my hair?"

"Again, we aren't sure, but taking hair from his victims is part of his ritual. He is clearly mentally and emotionally disturbed."

Officer Timmins handed Ward the police report and the composite drawing. Ward expected the murder's face to be rough, even cruel, but instead, though the sketch was quickly drawn, the man's face reminded Ward of a finely sculptured head of a young Roman general he had seen in a museum. The face suggested a clever and crafty mind—someone supremely confident. Ward slid the drawing under the police report so it wouldn't distract Janet Gibbons.

Officer Timmins began by summarizing the report taken the evening Ms. Gibbons was attacked. "Miss Gibbons met our suspect at the Royal Ontario Museum of Art. She's an art student. He introduced himself as Henrik Stevron from Brussels and said he was an art dealer."

"What was the focus of the exhibit?" Ward asked.

Janet looked surprised at Ward's question. "It was a special exhibit of Pre-Raphaelite paintings and poetry. I was doing a paper on Waterhouse's painting The Lady of Shallot. The museum had a special exhibit and that's where I met my attacker."

"Did your attacker seem to be knowledgeable about this group of artists?"

"Oh, yes! He knew all about who made up this group and he seemed to know every painting and poem they produced. His knowledge was impressive."

Officer Timmins interrupted. "The name he gave to Miss Gibbons appears to be made up. We checked all dealers in Brussels. Henrik Stevron does not exist."

"And had you ever seen this man before?" Bull inquired.

Janet shifted uneasily in her chair. "No, I never met him. When the presentation at the museum was finished, he introduced himself and invited me to dinner. He told me he had seen me before. That confused me. I thought maybe he was talking about seeing me on campus, but he said he had seen me at a number of museum exhibits and was hoping to meet me. He said he admired my dedication to the greater ideals and that he was certain my beauty would please the gods. I laughed when he said that, and was flattered, but I had no idea what he meant. Strangely he seemed to know quite a bit about me."

"Did that bother you?"

"Yes. I started to feel uncomfortable and was sorry I had accepted his offer to dinner. When the dinner was over, he was to drive me home, but instead, he drove to High Park and attacked me." Janet paused, and then continued.

"As we drove into the park, he swung his arm out and hit me in the face with his fist." Janet pointed to her cut lip. "My head hit the passenger door and I was in a great deal of pain. Thank God I didn't pass out. He parked behind a building and dragged me to the back of the van and onto a mattress. He straddled me, pinning my arms under his legs. I starting screaming, but he remained very calm and kept saying that my beauty would please the gods. When he pulled the hair covering my forehead back and saw my birthmark, he went crazy. He called me a whore, a defiler. He reached for a knife and began slashing at my face. I grabbed his hand, and twisted it till he dropped the knife. That's when I heard a dog barking at the rear doors of the van. When I called out for help, he punched me several times in the face."

"How did he get the knife?" Bull asked.

"He had a bag hanging on the inside of the van near the mattress. He reached over and opened it; I saw the knives. He had at least a dozen of them, but they weren't ordinary knives. They were large and their handles were carved with designs. Some of the handles were shaped in the form of an animal's head. When he dropped the knife, I grabbed it and managed to cut him across the face. He yelled and fell to one side. I was able to open the door and jump out."

"Did he come after you?" Ward asked.

"No, but I think he would have if that man hadn't been there with his dog. All I remember is that when I stopped running and looked back, the van was racing up the street."

Peter Saunders

Chapter 33: Setting the Trap

It was Saturday morning and Ward had sat in room 315 of the New York Public Library for hours, pouring through prints of paintings by Waterhouse, Bouguereau, and Lord Leighton. O'Hare said that Neils, the suspected serial killer, had ranted on about how Modernism was destroying the reputations of these artists, the finest to walk the face of the earth. Private collectors were also to blame because they removed these masterpieces from public view, thereby weakening the impact the paintings were meant to have on all who viewed them. Although some of the artists were unfamiliar to Ward, he decided that perhaps their paintings would tell him something about the killer, something that might help formulate a plan for capturing him.

It was clear from the prints that Waterhouse loved and admired strong, sensuous, and alluring women. The depicted women seemed completely aware of the power their physical beauty had over men. The allure was clearly physical, but there was something else, something unspoken. As Ward turned page after page of prints, he kept thinking of the strange ritual the murderer performed on his victims. He cut their throats, folded their arms and tilted their heads back to expose their wounds for all to see. Clipped strands of their hair were taped over their eyes. It was as though the murderer was preparing their bodies and souls for the next world. History is filled with recorded ceremonies where the dead are prepared for their journey to the spiritual world. Flipping through notes he had taken when interviewing O'Hare, Ward found the odd remark their suspected killer made in one of his telephone calls to O'Hare: Natural beauty needs to be captured before the corruption begins. The gods demand it.

Ward stared at the sentences. All the murdered women were beautiful. If the beauty these women represented needed to be captured, could the ritual killings have been the murderer's insane attempt to do just that?

Once the sacrifice was complete, the murderer didn't seem interested in the bodies of his victims. In killing the women in their prime, perhaps in his disturbed mind, he thought he was preventing the aging process, thus capturing their beauty the way a painting is able to capture a subject's beauty for eternity. The women he chose were offerings to his imaginary god. The idea seemed crazy, but just crazy enough to be a possible motive for a deranged killer.

Before leaving the library, Ward made a call to the Fort Dix prison and asked if they would give O'Hare a message. Ward had a question only O'Hare could answer. When could they meet? By the time Ward arrived back at his apartment, he was surprised to find a message from the prison on his answering machine. O'Hare would see him the next day. There were also messages from Bull and Michelle. Ward decided that Bull would enjoy meeting the genius responsible for so many art heists.

Ward and Bull proceeded down a flight of metal stairs to the prison basement and from there down a long hallway. At the far end of the hall was the prison library. O'Hare was seated with two other inmates at a round metal table. When he saw Ward, he spoke briefly to his fellow inmates and they left.

"Ah, Mr. Emerson." He peered at Bull. "And who would this fine young man be?"

"O'Hare, meet Vincent Toolman. One of the best detectives this side of the Atlantic."

O'Hare seemed genuinely impressed. "Well, well! Coming from Mr. Emerson, that is quite a compliment. It is indeed a pleasure to meet you, Vincent." O'Hare's stood briefly as he shook Bull's hand. "Please sit down. I should add that it is a pleasure to meet you both as long as I am not the object of your hunt. You see, Vincent, professional thieves and detectives share the same rare qualities—intelligence and cunning. We are cut from the same cloth, but we have had, you might say, different tailors."

Bull laughed. "I never thought of it that way."

O'Hare smiled. "Now let me tell you, few people truly appreciate our gifts. When manners and intelligence lose their currency, it is a sorry time for the human race. A sorry time, I tell you. But I ramble on. How can I help you gentlemen?"

Ward shared with O'Hare his suspicions as to why their suspected murderer might be killing, why he was driven to murder. He filled O'Hare in on what happened to Janet Gibbons in Canada.

O'Hare shook his head. "You said she had a birthmark on her forehead, and he went crazy when he saw that?"

"Yes, that's what Ms. Gibbons told us."

O'Hare stood up and walked over to the guard standing by the door and whispered something to him. The guard nodded, stepped outside and closed the door. O'Hare sat down again. "The women he sacrifices seem to him to be perfect specimens of female beauty. When he saw a birthmark, he realized he had made a terrible error. His victim was imperfect and he could not offer her to his gods."

"I believe the man you spoke to regarding art heists is the serial killer who attacked the woman in Toronto and murdered my wife and those other women. I want to set a trap, and capture this guy. We'll let the authorities cross-examine him. He needs to be eliminated as a suspect, and I think I know how to draw him out. You told me that our suspect is furious that many of the paintings he worships are making their way into the hands of private collectors and their collections are rarely seen again by the general public."

"Yes, the man I spoke to, believed the paintings by the artists he worshipped were meant to be displayed to inspire the public to greater ideals. In his mind, private collectors were the enemy."

Bull jumped in. "But I thought I read somewhere that the artists he worships are not popular anymore. I mean even if their paintings were displayed, how many people would be influenced or consider their works worth looking at?"

O'Hare smiled. "Mr. Toolman, I see you have a fine mind, just like your partner. Your comment gets at another key point. Generally, the more times people see a work, the more likely the reputation of the artist will grow. My contact is aware that a work locked in a private collection can be nearly forgotten. It's truly sad."

Ward joined in, "What if we let it be known that one of the paintings he worships is destined to disappear into a private collection? Would he make a move to prevent that from happening? Can you think of a painting that fits that description?"

"I can think of several," O'Hare said.

"My wife worked for the Hoeysunder Art Museum and Auction House in Connecticut. We became good friends with the owners. Barbara knew someone at all the major auction houses and museums. I believe we could spread the word through the auction houses that a particular painting is to be auctioned off to private collectors at the Hoeysunder Museum."

O'Hare leaned back and considered Ward's suggestion. "Yes, I know the Hoeysunders, especially Gerald. He knows a masterpiece when he sees one. The family has handled some major works over the years, and to tell the truth, I did not have the heart to steal any of their paintings." O'Hare smiled. "I doubt I could sneak one of my copies past Gerald. He has a wonderful eye for originals. I will talk to him and explain the situation. I'm sure he'll cooperate."

Ward smiled. "So if a painting which has been in a private collection were to be put to auction, it would offer our suspect a rare opportunity to steal the painting before it disappears again. Do you agree such a situation might draw him out?"

"Only if it was one of the masterpieces."

"Which painting might have the power to draw him into our net?"

"Well, if I were going to set this trap, my first choice would be Waterhouse's final portrayal of Ophelia. He depicts a mature Ophelia looking directly at the viewer. She is captured just before she steps into her watery grave. In a way, Waterhouse has rescued her voluptuous beauty, captured it before her sacrifice. Yes, The Last Ophelia would draw this man out if he felt she needed to be rescued from the grave of private collectors. Of course, we are not sure that my contact is the man you're looking for, but I guess one way to find out is as you suggest. I could contact him and recommend he lift this painting."

Ward took a deep breath. "So I need to find who has this painting and persuade them to participate in our sting?"

Gallery of the Chosen

O'Hare chuckled and stood up. "Today is your lucky day, Mr. Emerson, for haven't I been encouraged by one of my benefactors to give you a gift. For the life of me, haven't I been sitting here, mulling over just how I would do that. And like a miracle, in you walk to give me the answer I've been looking for."

"A gift? What kind of a gift?"

O'Hare paused, measuring his words carefully. "A rare and precious gift, Mr. Emerson. A truly rare and precious gift."

"And what do I have to do to earn this gift?"

O'Hare shook his head. "That's the wonder and glory of it. You have already earned it."

"Is this some kind of a trick?"

O'Hare cut him off. "Oh, no. There is no card up my sleeve, no rabbit hiding in the false bottom of my hat. This gift is genuine. I will attest to that personally. But there are three conditions."

Ward leaned forward and met his eyes. "There always are. I can't pull any strings for you. You know that, don't you?"

"I ask nothing for myself in return. This gift is offered for kindnesses rendered."

Bull jumped in and turned to Ward. "I'm confused. What is he talking about?"

Ward responded. "What's the gift, Patrick, and what are the conditions?"

"I happen to know where Waterhouse's last painting of Ophelia is, and I believe I can persuade the owner of the original to pretend his prize possession must be put up to auction."

"Why would whoever owns the painting agree to do that?"

O'Hare laughed. "Let's just say we have had a long and prosperous history together in building his collection over the years. Put bluntly, he owes me. But, you must not ask any questions about who holds the painting. Agreed?"

Ward thought for a moment. "Agreed. And the second condition?"

"The painting is to be returned to its owner through me."

"Yes, I can agree to that. But I still don't understand why you would do this for me? I don't know how to thank you."

O'Hare look surprised. "Lord, it's not me you need to be thanking. I'm just the messenger. But I'm sure your benefactor appreciates what this means to you."

O'Hare reached out and shook Bull's hand and stood. "My time here is up. I've enjoyed your visit. Someone will contact you about the painting. Once they have it, I will let it be known through our network that this rare painting has surfaced and is to be auctioned at the Hoeysunder Museum. I will contact the museum and arrange for the delivery of the painting and suggest a date and publicity for the auction, which will be cancelled, should our suspect decide not to lift the painting. And I will suggest my contact lift the Waterhouse painting on a specific evening prior to the auction, and at a specific time. Our suspect will be given a map of the museum's floor plan showing the suggested route he should follow once he gets into the museum. You will receive a similar map so you will know when and where our suspect will enter and seek out the painting.

"I suggest you pay a visit to the museum soon and make sure you understand the layout of the floors, stairwells and storage rooms. Remember, it will be evening and dark when the attempted robbery takes place. Someone will contact you when everything is set, but I would not involve the police until you have captured your man. Keep them at a distance if you can. It is amazing how word travels. It will be your task to grab the suspect. I cannot promise you that he is the person you are looking for, but at least you will be able to remove him as a suspect."

"You said there were three conditions? What's the third?"

"If the person you nab is not your serial killer, you must find a way to charge him with only a minor offense. Our lawyers will take care of the rest. They will have him freed. Can you agree to that?"

Ward took a deep breath and considered his options. "It will be tricky, but I believe we can arrange that."

"Good. Vincent, have you visited the Hoeysunder Museum?"

"No, I haven't had the pleasure."

"It will not disappoint you, artistically speaking. The Hoeysunder is a lovely museum, a 20th Century Beau-Arts building, a true work of art. Make sure you visit the garden courtyard when you go. Mr. Emerson, I hope you find the peace you have been looking for in their courtyard garden. It has given peace to many troubled souls."

Chapter 34: Encounter at the Hoeysunder Museum

The Hoeysunder Museum is a two-story 1912 Beaux-Arts building nestled inside an expansive park of trees, gardens and ponds. Bull investigated the museum's collections and discovered that many of the artists Neils worshiped were represented in a room dedicated to "Art Depicting Life." On the coming weekend, the museum was having a lecture and discussion of the collection. Ward had a feeling Neils might attend, so when Saturday came, he and Michelle and Bull headed out to the lecture. The room set aside for lectures doubled as an auction hall and today it was crowded. Nearly every one of the seventy-five seats was occupied.

Ward whispered to Bull, "I'm going to walk around and see if I can spot Neils." Ward moved slowly to the back of the room looking for a man with scars across his face, but no one seemed to fit the profile. After circling the room, he rejoined Bull and Michelle. "I didn't see anyone who looks like our suspect, but I'll keep checking. When the lecture is over, we'll familiarized ourselves with the museum layout."

Ward pulled out the map Patrick O'Hare had sent him. He studied it until the lecturer began his presentation and then the map was put away. The speaker concluded his remarks an hour later and invited everyone to join him in the atrium for light refreshments. The audience applauded and hurried from the room. Once in the atrium most of those attending went directly to the bar and ordered cocktails. Waiters began circling the room with small sandwiches on silver trays. Bull followed one busy waiter who carried an abundance of sandwiches, but the waiter seemed determined to deny Bull a share of the culinary treasures.

Across the room, Mr. Alexander Firth, the director of the museum, chatted with Ward and Michelle. They stood in front of an exhibit not far from a vaulted recess displaying a collection of 18th Century paintings. Above the recess was a balcony off the second floor where a tall, well-dressed, bearded man now stood gazing down at Michelle.

After a few minutes, he exited the balcony and entered the atrium. With a cocktail in one hand and his other hand tucked in a jacket pocket, he slowly made his way toward Ward, Michelle and Firth. He stopped a few feet from Michelle as a heavyset young man joined Ward and the others. The man turned away, and pretended to be examining a display of artists' sketches of their masterpieces.

As he studied the sketches, he kept glancing at Michelle, studying her face, her posture, and the attractive dress accenting her lean body. He looked closely at her hair, tied back from her face, revealing her beautiful neck.

This woman would please, he thought, and quickly removed a small camera from his pocket and snapped a few pictures of her. He was preparing to take one more picture when suddenly, as if someone had called to her from across the room, Michelle turned in time to notice her picture being taken.

Her eyes met the stranger's gaze as he dropped the camera back in his pocket. He smiled, then turned and moved away. An intense shiver ran through Michelle's body. She knew she had looked into the eyes of Barbara's murderer. She grabbed Ward's arm and whispered what had just taken place. Ward and Bull immediately began searching for the man with the camera, but he was nowhere to be seen. Ward ran out the front door and onto the street in time to see a car pull away. He stared at the empty street, his heart racing. *Please, Lord, not again.*

###

Michelle's encounter with Neils unnerved her. Each evening after that incident, either Ward or Bull drove her from work to her sister's house. They agreed that if she were the serial killer's next target, they would make it impossible for him to get her alone. And just for insurance, Ward gave Michelle a colt .45 revolver that was easily concealed and could be used at close range. By the second week, Bull thought a car was following him as he drove Michelle to her sister's house. He drove past the house and dropped Michelle at Ward's apartment. The car did not show up again.

Gallery of the Chosen

A week passed, then two, then three. They heard nothing from O'Hare. Meanwhile, Ward and Bull spent their time carefully studying the layout of the Hoeysunder Museum. In preparation for what they hoped would be a face-to-face encounter, they returned to the museum several times, memorizing every step of the route O'Hare had outlined for Neils. The big question was would Neils show up and would he follow O'Hare's instructions once he entered the museum? O'Hare promised someone would contact Ward when all was set, but no one called. Had the plan fallen through? Ward remembered Professor Rapin's comment about O'Hare: don't believe anything he says if he does talk. He is very, very convincing, but he's a major liar.

Back at his apartment, Ward made an enlarged copy of the map O'Hare had sent, pinning it on a poster board next to the victims' profiles. One evening he and Bull sat looking at the pictures. Bull noticed the worried expression on Ward's face.

"Don't worry, I know the route," Bull insisted. "I could follow that path with my eyes closed."

Ward smiled but his drawn face suggested he was still worried. "We can't afford to mess up," he said.

Toward the end of the fourth week, when the two men returned from doing some research, Ward hung up his coat and went into his bedroom, returning with a large wooden box, which he set on the table. Opening the lid, he removed his Colt .32 caliber semi-automatic pistol, the weapon issued by the New York Police Department for their detective squad. Bull watched as Ward loaded the gun. In all the time they had been together, only once had Ward carried a gun.

"Ward?"

"Yeah?" He filled the last chamber but didn't look up.

"Don't you think I should be armed? I've taken training courses on firearms, especially small handguns."

Ward looked at Bull. "Yes, I think you should carry your gun. You're ready. Just be careful." He reached into the box, removed another Colt .32 and handed it to his partner. "I hope you don't have to use it, but if you do need to protect yourself, don't hesitate to pull the trigger, understand?"

Before Bull could answer, the telephone rang. Ward grabbed the receiver. "Yes, this is Ward Emerson speaking." He reached for his pen and paper and jotted information down.

###

O'Hare's instructions were crystal clear, but he listed two different days when his contact might try to lift the Waterhouse painting which had already been delivered to the museum. Publicity announcing the auction had appeared in all the art magazines and a special flyer was mailed to prospective buyers. Ward had secured keys for the museum's side door and the basement storage room where the painting was to be placed. They had developed a simple plan on how they would capture their murderer. The storage room had no windows and only one door. It was made of metal and was secured with a padlock on the outside. O'Hare had arranged for the alarm system to be disabled and for the thief to be supplied with one key to the museum's side door and another to open the storeroom's padlock. The plan was simple; Ward and Bull would hide in the room across the hall from the storage room. Once their suspect was inside the storeroom, they would lock him in from the outside and wait until the police arrived.

An hour before closing time on the first date O'Hare suggested the painting be lifted, Ward and Bull took their positions and waited. Empty crates were piled high near one wall with just enough room for two men to hide from sight. The hours dragged by as the men waited, but no one came.

On the second night, Ward and Bull again took their positions and waited: one o'clock, two o'clock, and three o'clock. They took turns keeping watch. At 4 a.m. Bull dozed off while Ward sat waiting, his pistol in hand. Suddenly he heard a soft rattling sound upstairs. Ward nudged Bull.

They waited, with time passing slowly, but there were no more sounds. The two men relaxed, still sheltered by the crates around them. And then they heard another sound. Someone had entered the museum and was walking through the rooms upstairs making sure the museum was empty.

Gallery of the Chosen

Ward and Bull hid behind the crates and waited. Footsteps descended the stairs to the basement, slowly advancing down the hallway. Whoever had come down the stairs, stopped across the hall from where Ward and Bull were hiding. Ward signaled Bull to hold his position, and Bull, taking a deep breath, nodded, his gun readied. Someone was opening the padlock across the hall. They heard the storeroom door opening and the click of lights switched on. Whoever entered the room quickly walked around then clicked off the lights and closed the door.

Bull started to move from behind the crates, but Ward stopped him. Suddenly the door to their room opened. A sliver of light spread across the floor as lights were switched on. Someone entered their room walked slowly around and paused briefly on the other side of the crates sheltering the two detectives. Bull's hand, that held his gun, shook and his heart raced. Whoever had entered the room moved on, turned off the lights and left. Footsteps climbed the stairs to the first floor.

Ward gave Bull's sleeve a tug and together they made their way in the dark to the storeroom door. They could hear someone on the first floor and then the sound of the museum's side door slamming shut. A car engine started up. They waited in silence. After ten minutes, Ward and Bull flipped on the lights and walked to the back of the storeroom where the Waterhouse painting had been placed behind three other paintings. The painting was still there. A burlap cloth had been wrapped around the painting and tied with heavy cord. A label indicating the painting's title was attached to the burlap so it could not be confused with other paintings.

"I don't get it. Why didn't he take the painting?" Bull sat on a stool wiping his face with his handkerchief. "Whoever came in here probably wanted to check that the museum was empty and the painting really was here. That means there are two men working this heist. Keep that gun handy." The floor upstairs suddenly creaked. Ward shot a glance at Bull as he turned off the lights, and together they moved behind a large screen. In a few minutes, the storeroom door opened and the light was switched on.

Whoever entered made his way directly to the painting. Ward waited for the second man to enter, but no one came. The only sound was that of the man already in the room, removing the Waterhouse painting. Ward stepped from behind the screen, blocking the passageway, his gun pointed directly at the thief's heart. It was the man Michelle had seen taking her picture. Although he was bearded, Ward could see the deep scars Janet Gibbons made as she defended herself.

"Neils, you're not going anywhere with the Waterhouse painting."

Neils stared at Ward, a shocked expression on his face. "How do you know who I am?"

"Never mind. I have been looking for you for a long, long time and now we finally meet."

While Ward was talking, Bull moved from behind the screen and stood beside Ward, his gun ready. Suddenly, a voice called from upstairs. "Neils? Is everything all right?"

Neils responded, "We have company down here, two cops with guns."

Ward whispered to Bull, "Keep your gun on Neils, I'll take care of the guy upstairs." Ward slipped out of the room and headed for the stairs.

Upstairs, Ward moved slowly through the museum's rooms, his gun ready. Suddenly a bullet flew over his head. He turned in time to see his assailant standing on a staircase, his gun poised. Ward got off a shot that hit his attacker in the shoulder, but another shot from the assailant barely missed Ward's arm. Ward shot back. The attacker fell, rolled down the stairs, and lay motionless. At that moment, a series of gunshots rang out from the storage room below. Ward quickly headed back. When he stepped into the storeroom, he froze. Neils had a knife at Bull's throat and had pulled him to the back of the room. The Waterhouse painting remained near the entrance, close to Ward's feet.

"Drop your gun and kick it to me or I'll cut your friend's throat," Neils demanded.

Ward dropped his gun and kicked it toward Neils. It stopped at Bull's feet. Ward noticed a crowbar resting on one of the crates. "Neils, you don't want to kill my friend. His life is of no value to you. Your friend upstairs is dead. He can't help you now." Ward grabbed the Waterhouse painting still wrapped in burlap and moved it closer to Neils.

"What are you doing? Leave that painting alone." Neils seemed confused.

Ward kept moving the painting closer to Neils. "This is what you want, this masterpiece by Waterhouse."

Neils eyed Ward cautiously, "What do you know about Waterhouse?"

"I know he was a genius and was misunderstood by society. I know that his painting of Ophelia was to be locked away, robbing the public from viewing his masterpiece. But you were trying to stop that, weren't you?"

Neils nodded. "Yes, I only want the painting because the gods demand that I protect the ideal Ophelia represents."

Ward moved the painting still closer. "I know that. And those women you sacrificed, you were saving their beauty, too. Isn't that right?"

Neils nodded. "Those women had no idea their beauty was sacred. They were all whores, all caught up in their own weaknesses. I saved them, but no one understands." Neils suddenly tightened his grip on Bull and pressed his knife harder against Bull's throat. A small trickle of blood appeared.

Ward's muscles tightened. "Oh, you're wrong, Neils. I understand completely the important role you played. Those women were beautiful, but you saw something greater than their beauty. Let my friend go and you can leave with the painting."

Neils looked as if he might accept Ward's offer, but then suddenly he shook his head. "Don't try anything because I would enjoy killing this pig."

Ward knew he was still too far away to stop Neils from killing Bull. He needed to distract the murderer.

"We're making no deal," Neils said. "I have to kill you both. I can't take chances."

In desperation, Ward grabbed the crowbar and positioned it over the Waterhouse painting. "Neils, let my friend go or I'll destroy the painting, so help me God." Ward swung the crowbar viciously against one of the crates, smashing a hole in its side. Neils seemed stunned.

"Let him go, Neils, and you save the painting and get to leave. Kill my partner and I destroy the Waterhouse and you will go to jail for murder. The gods will hate you, and all your good work will be for nothing. What good is he, they'll say? Drop the knife, Neils. Save the painting and the gods will praise you."

Neils' hand holding the knife shook and when it did, more blood ran down Bull's shirt.

Ward lifted the crowbar a second time and swung it viciously against one side of the Waterhouse painting's frame. Splinters flew everywhere.

"Let him go, Neils. It's either my friend or the painting. We both know which is more valuable." Ward raised his arm and was about to deliver another blow when Neils screamed, "No, don't destroy it. I'll let the fool go, but leave the painting."

Neils dropped his knife and reached down to grab the gun on the floor. Bull kicked it to Ward and pulled away from Neils. Ward grabbed the gun, aimed and pulled the trigger. Neils' body recoiled backward, pressing against a pile of crates. Ward moved toward him. "This one is for Barbara and all the other women." Ward pulled the trigger again and Neils fell to the floor.

Bull grabbed a piece of burlap and pressed it against his throat till the bleeding stopped. Meanwhile, Ward went upstairs, called the police and returned. Together they sat on crates looking at Neils' dead body.

"Are you okay?" Ward asked.

Bull checked the bleeding. "It's almost stopped, but I don't understand what this character sees as so important about this painting. I looked it up in the library, but it doesn't seem that special."

Ward smiled. "Well, I'm no expert, but many critics feel this is a masterpiece. Here, let's look." Ward carefully unwrapped the burlap from around the painting, and stared in disbelief. He started laughing. "Son of a bitch!"

Bull looked at the painting. "Hey, that's not the Waterhouse painting."

Ward chuckled as he gazed at the name Valerie painted in beautiful colors across the canvas. Underneath the name was the inscription:

"If ever any beauty I did see,
Which I desired, and got, 'twas but a dream of thee."
J.D.

"No, it's not the Waterhouse painting. O'Hare has pulled a fast one on all of us. I will have some words with him when I see him."

Bull scratched his head. "Do you know who Valerie is?"

Ward smiled, "Yes, Valerie is O'Hare's one and only love."

Peter Saunders

Chapter 35: Elizabeth's Final Wish

On a warm spring Friday, Ward, Michelle and Bull stood at a respectful distance from the large Dwyer headstone. Susan and Angela King were next to Paul Dwyer and their priest as workmen dug deep into the soil. Angela had her arm around Paul who held one hand over his eyes, trying to hide his tears. Susan stood beside him, holding his other hand. His good friend Rafael was nearby.

Johnny Lynks' remains were slowly lifted from the grave and lowered into a new casket waiting on a flatbed truck. Officials from the cemetery and the Attorney General's office were present as required by law. Once all the papers were signed, Lynks' remains were driven away and the workers began refilling the grave.

Susan joined Ward, Michelle and Bull and hugged each of them. "We can't thank you enough for everything you've done. Elizabeth's final wish has been granted. Do you have any idea what will become of Lynks' remains?"

"He'll be buried in upstate New York. You need to thank Rafael for helping us clear all the legal hurdles."

Susan looked back at her family members as they made their way to their cars. "I better go now." She walked a few steps and then turned back. "Ward, I've thought about your advice that I should have let sleeping dogs lie. Did you really want me to do that?"

Ward smiled, "No, Susan. That was a test to see how much this really meant to you."

"And did I pass your test?"

Ward took Michelle's hand and winked at Bull. "Oh, yes. When you decided to keep going regardless of the consequences, we knew this was a very special assignment."

Susan smiled. "Elizabeth thanks all of you." Susan waved then joined her family.

Ward, Michelle and Bull turned and walked away.

"Any chance we can stop at the donut shop across the street?" Bull whispered.

"You want food?" Ward looked surprised.

Michelle laughed at the expression on his face, and then gave him a hug. "If you aren't hungry, Ward, maybe you and I can find something else to do."

Ward studied her face, then handed Bull some money. "Take the rest of the day off. Buy yourself a dozen donuts, and then take the taxi home. I don't want to see you before Monday."

Peter Saunders

Dr. Saunders is a retired professor of literature who has over thirty years teaching at colleges and universities in the United States, Canada and overseas.

He has authored a writing textbook, short stories and academic articles on literature and teaching.

He lives in Ohio with his wife Joan, their dog Pepe, and two cats, Captain Quirk and Flambee

Peter Saunders

Starry Night Publishing

Everyone has a story...

Don't spend your life trying to get published! Don't tolerate rejection! Don't do all the work and allow the publishing companies reap the rewards!

Millions of independent authors like you, are making money, publishing their stories now. Our technological know-how will take the headaches out of getting published. Let "Starry Night Publishing dot Com" take care of the hard parts, so you can focus on writing. You simply send us your Word document and we do the rest. It really is that simple!

The big companies want to publish only "celebrity authors," not the average book-writer. It's almost impossible for first-time authors to get published today. This has led many authors to go the self-publishing route. Until recently, this was considered "vanity-publishing." You spent large sums of your money, to get twenty copies of your book, to give to relatives at Christmas, just so you could see your name on the cover. Now, however, the self-publishing industry allows authors to get published in a timely fashion, retain the rights to your work, keeping up to seventy-percent of your royalties, instead of the traditional ten-percent.

Peter Saunders

We've opened up the gates, allowing you inside the world of publishing. While others charge you as much as ten-thousand dollars for a publishing package, we charge less than three-hundred dollars to cover proofreading, copyright, ISBN, and distribution costs. Do you really want to spend all your time formatting, converting, designing a cover, and then promoting your book, because no one else will?

Our editors are professionals, able to create a top-notch book that you will be proud of. Becoming a published author is supposed to be fun, not a hassle.

At Starry Night Publishing, you submit your work, we proofread it, create a professional-looking cover, a table of contents, compile your text and images into the appropriate format, convert your files for eReaders, take care of copyright information, assign an ISBN, allow you to keep one-hundred-percent of your rights, distribute your story worldwide on Amazon, Barnes & Noble and many other retailers, and write you a check for your royalties. There are no other hidden fees involved! You don't pay extra for a cover, or proofreading. You will never pay to keep your book in print. We promise! Everything is included! You even get a free copy of your book and unlimited discount copies.

In twelve short months, we've published more than three-hundred books, compared to the major publishing houses which only add an average of six new titles per year. We will publish your fiction, or non-fiction books about anything, and look forward to reading your stories and sharing them with the world.

We sincerely hope that you will join the growing Starry Night Publishing family, become a published author and gain the world-wide exposure that you deserve. You deserve to succeed. Success comes to those who make opportunities happen, not those who wait for opportunities to happen. You just have to try. Thanks for joining us on our journey.

www.starrynightpublishing.com

www.facebook.com/starrynightpublishing/

Made in the USA
San Bernardino, CA
06 April 2015